Kaua'i Me a River

JoAnn Bassett

First published by JoAnn Bassett
Green Valley, AZ 85614
http://www.joannbassett.com
***
***
Printed in the United States of America

Also by JoAnn Bassett:

"THE ISLANDS OF ALOHA MYSTERY SERIES"
Maui Widow Waltz
Livin' Lahaina Loca
Lana'i of the Tiger

MAI TAI BUTTERFLY

Discover the latest titles by JoAnn Bassett at
http://www.joannbassett.com

ISBN: 1484198921
ISBN-13: 978-1484198926

This one's for Diana and Roger Paul.
Mahalo nui loa for including us in your Kaua'i *hau'oli la hanau* celebration.

1

Up until noon I'd avoided thinking about my birthday. But then the mail carrier came in and thumped a stack of bills and bridal catalogs down on my desk and waved a white business envelope under my nose.

"You know anybody this name?" growled the mailman. It wasn't actually a mail "man", but a mail "lady," but not by much.

I stared at the envelope. The name I go by is Pali Moon. But the letter in question was addressed to my birth name—a lengthy string of celestial gibberish that my 1970's hippie parents must've considered real 'far out.' I never use my real name. In fact, I can count on one hand the number of people who even know it. But there it was.

"Oh, this must be a friend messing with me," I said. I hoped the mail carrier hadn't noticed my eyes bug out when I'd read my birth name and put two and two together and realized this letter had come on my birthday. Even under the pressure of her scowl I managed to come up with an almost believable fib. "My college roommate and I took Astronomy together and we came up with crazy handles for each other."

"I didn' know," she said. "I almost throw it in the 'return' pile but I think I betta ask. We gotta do the *da kine* job, ya know."

"*Mahalo,* and sorry about the confusion. I'll tell her to knock it off."

The return address was a lawyer's office in Hanalei, Kaua'i. I assumed it was a lawyer because, honestly, who else but a lawyer would use the word 'Esquire' after their name? What does the word even mean? It conjures up an image of a chap in top hat and leather breeches gripping a riding crop and clopping through town on a chestnut mare. Not exactly the image I had of the residents of the little town of Hanalei on the north shore of Kaua'i. Hanalei's enduring claim to fame is it was the inspiration for a hippie-days ode to *pakalolo*—marijuana—called "Puff the Magic Dragon."

It took me a minute to calm down after the mail carrier left. Why would a lawyer in Kaua'i send me birthday greetings?

***

My birthday has always been a downer. When I was a kid, I didn't like it because it fell in mid-June when school was out for the summer. I never got to wear the crumpled Burger King crown in class and I never got to ask the girls in my room to a sleepover. Now that I'm a fully-functioning adult, my birthday bums me out for a different reason. It's not the getting older. I don't mind getting older. I turned thirty-five this year and it's fine. I'm a lot more confident at thirty-five than I ever was at twenty-five. What's depressing is my birthday shines a light on my almost complete lack of family, or *ohana*. In

Hawaii, *ohana* is the backbone of society. But aside from a half-brother on the mainland, I don't share even a smidgen of DNA with another soul on the planet.

The good news is I'm usually too busy in June to sit around fretting about my birthday. I'm the owner of "Let's Get Maui'd," a wedding planning business in Pa'ia, Maui. June is my second-busiest month; December being number one. For the past couple of years I've managed to dodge my 'special day' by concentrating on pleasing fussy brides on their 'special day.' And that's fine with me.

***

Soon after the mail arrived my best friend, Farrah Milton, called me on my cell. "Happy birthday, Pali. When are you coming over to get your present?" Farrah works right next door to my shop, but she has to call and ask me to come over if she wants to see me. She runs the Gadda da Vida Grocery and she can't leave the store for even a couple of minutes. The residents of Pa'ia are prone to 'the munchies' at all times of the day or night. A locked door between a guy and the Snickers bar he's craving is an invitation to major property damage.

"You free now?" I said.

"Not free, but the price is dropping fast."

"Okay. I'll be right over."

I went in through the front. There's an annoying little tinkly bell on the front door that announces anyone coming or going. I used to come in through the back to circumvent the bell, but Farrah got jumped last year so now I'm careful to avoid startling her.

"Hey, *hau'oli la hanau!*" she said, wishing me happy birthday. She dashed around the counter and gripped me in a tight hug. Farrah isn't fat, at least by American standards, but she isn't wiry like me, either. If I were making a stick figure of Farrah I'd draw her middle section as sort of an oval. I'd put in a sideways "8" to emphasize the girly parts. She has major "girls" that are hard to ignore.

"You don't look a day over thirty-four," she said with a wink. "You and Hatch going out tonight?"

"No, he's working today. He's planning something great for tomorrow, though."

"Well, I've got something for you right now." She handed me a small box wrapped in newspaper and tied with a length of dried palm frond. "Totally recycled wrapping. Cool, eh? But no worries, I didn't re-gift you or nuthin'. I picked your present out special."

I tore off the wrapping. Inside was a jeweler's box. I don't wear jewelry so I hesitated. I needed to prepare myself to say, '*Oh, I love it*' when I really didn't.

I popped up the lid. Inside was a necklace with a gleaming Tahitian pearl strung on a black rubbery cord. For someone who isn't into jewelry it was a great compromise.

"Wow, it's perfect," I said truthfully. "Really gorgeous." The large pearl was a deep smoky gray. When I held it up to the light it shimmered with jade green and rosy pink highlights.

"Okay, like I get it that you don't dig jewelry, but your birthstone is pearl. And I thought the black rubber thing makes it more like an amulet than a necklace. And you know how I feel about amulets."

Farrah's chosen lifestyle puts a capital "C" on the words 'counter-culture'. She owns an impressive assemblage of Tarot cards, Ouija boards, crystals, pyramids and charms. Her collection of all things paranormal is along the lines of a foodie collecting cookbooks or a cat lover filling her house with cat calendars, kitty T-shirts and feline figurines.

"*Mahalo* for the beautiful amulet," I said. "I'm going to put it on right now."

She helped me with the clasp and we hugged again. A customer came in so we said our good-byes and I slipped out the back. In the fuss over my birthday present I'd totally forgotten to tell her about the lawyer letter.

***

I took the unopened envelope home with me that night. Farrah had been busy with customers for the rest of the afternoon, so I hadn't been able to go back over and show it to her. I wanted to open it with a friend standing by to offer moral support. Next to Farrah, my roommate Steve is just such a friend. From the day he moved in we've been way more than just roommates. We're close. Not in the way you might expect a boy/girl thing to go, but close like brother and sister. A couple of years ago when he responded to my 'roommate wanted' notice I'd balked. I was a bit leery of taking on a guy as a house mate. I didn't need the aggravation of sexual tension and double entendres with my morning coffee. Luckily, Steve cleared things up right away.

"Uh, are you in favor of gay marriage?" he'd asked after I'd given him a short tour of my three bedroom, two bath house in Hali'imaile.

"Well, yeah. I'm a wedding planner. I'm pretty much in favor of any kind of marriage there is."

"No, what I mean is, I'm gay. So would you find it offensive if I had friends, you know, like gay friends, visit me here at the house?"

"You mean like sleep-overs?"

"Maybe."

"Look, I don't care what you do in the privacy of your own room. I only care that you obey the law, keep the noise down and clean up after yourself."

"You know guys like me sort of hold the patent on clean," he'd said. "You want to check out my car? You could eat sushi off the floor mats."

"Got it. So, I guess my next line is '*Ho'okipa* to your new home.' That is, if you think you'd like to live here with me."

He hugged me. And that was the start of a beautiful friendship.

On my birthday night I parked my decrepit green Geo Metro on the street and came up the front steps. I rarely use the front door, but since it was a special occasion I thought I'd get festive.

"Hey," yelled Steve. "I'm in the kitchen making you a fabulous dinner. I hope you weren't expecting a surprise party."

"Thanks but once a year is enough for me."

Steve had organized a big blow-out party when I'd been released from witness protection right before

Christmas. It'd been fun—the party, not witness protection—but I was glad he'd stifled the urge to go for an encore after only six months.

"I'm pulling out all the stops, girl," he said as I came into the kitchen. "Steven hinted he'd like to be invited, but I told him I wanted to give you my full attention."

"I still think it's funny your boyfriend's name is Steven. Do you both turn around when someone at the Ball and Chain calls your name?"

He looked puzzled. "No. Because his name is Steven and mine is Steve. I think I can recognize my own name when I hear it."

"Ooh, touchy," I said. "Sounds like this topic's come up before. Sorry. Anyway, speaking of names, get a load of this." I handed him the still-sealed envelope. Steve was one of the handful of people who knew my real name.

"What's this? Looks like it's from a lawyer," he said.

"Yeah. A lawyer on Kaua'i."

"Weren't you born on Kaua'i? Maybe it's something to do with your mom."

My mother had been a 1970's hippie who'd lived at Taylor Camp, a hippie haven on the North Shore. She died when I was five years old. My little brother and I were taken in by her best friend, a woman we called Auntie Mana. Auntie moved us to Maui to be closer to her extended family. As a single mom with three teenagers of her own and now two little *hanai* kids— that's what Hawaiians call foster kids—Auntie Mana needed all the help she could get.

"I don't know. It's been almost thirty years. You'd think anything to do with my mom would've been cleared up by now."

"Why haven't you opened it?"

"I guess I'm afraid of what it might say."

"Do you want me to do it?" He pulled a paring knife from the knife block on the counter.

I nodded.

"Sheesh, you've got a black belt in martial arts and you're scared of a piece of paper," Steve said in his *tsk-tsk* voice. "Maybe you've got 'pulpuslacerataphobia'."

"What the heck is that?"

"Fear of paper cuts. Look it up, it's a real word."

He slit the envelope and pulled out the letter. It was a single sheet. From what I could see, it didn't look like there was much writing on it.

"Hmm" Steve said when he was finished reading. "Confucius say: *You are about to embark on a long journey.*"

"Long journey?"

"Well, I guess a trip to a neighbor island would be a long journey for Confucius," he said. "They didn't have airplanes back then, you know."

"Give me that."

Steve handed me the letter.

I read it. When I finished, I was even more confused than before.

2

Sure enough, the letter was from a law office. The attorney who'd sent it wasn't the same person as the name on the return address, however. The signature was that of one Valentine Fabares, and she didn't use the honorific "Esquire" after her name but rather "Attorney-at-Law."

The message was brief. I'd been summoned to Hanalei to attend a meeting regarding an "urgent family matter" on Wednesday, June 27th. Since I had no family to speak of except my little brother, I figured it must be a mistake.

I looked at the clock. It was six-thirty in Maui, which made it nine-thirty at night in San Francisco. Probably too late to call an acquaintance but not too late to pester a family member.

"Hey, Jeff," I said when he answered. I always resented that Jeff had a normal name. He had a different father than I, so either his dad was less hippie-trippy than mine, or my mother had learned her lesson and she'd insisted on a name that didn't sound like two stoners naming their kid after enjoying two joints of *pakalolo* and a tab of peyote. Jeff had the same last name as my mom,

Warner. Hard to imagine a more normal name than Jeff Warner.

"Hey, Pali. How's it going? Everything okay?" Jeff and I are what I'd call "arm's length" siblings. We both care about each other, but we don't make keeping in touch a high priority.

"It's all good. I'm calling about something I got in the mail today," I said.

"Yeah? What is it?" His voice sounded as if he was waiting for me to say something funny. "Oh, I get it. Today's your birthday and I forgot to send you a card. Sorry."

"No, that's not it. I got a letter from a lawyer on Kaua'i. Did you get one too?"

"No, but it'd take longer to get here. What's it say?"

I told him about the meeting in Hanalei on the twenty-seventh.

"Seems I haven't been invited," he said. A beat went by and he said, "Pali? Who's it addressed to?" It was as if he was two steps ahead of me. Jeff works at the Lawrence Livermore Laboratory in California. He's literally a rocket scientist. He's been two steps ahead of me since he was three years old.

"The name that shall not be named."

"Huh. Well, there's a clue for you right there."

"Yeah, maybe. Anyway, how're you doing?" I said. It didn't feel right to just ask him about the letter and hang up; especially since it was my birthday. We chatted for about ten minutes and then Jeff said he had to be at work by six so he better get to bed.

"We should talk more often," he said.

"Yeah, we should."

"Oh, and happy birthday, Pali. I'll let you know if I get a letter like yours."

I hung up feeling good I'd talked to Jeff, but also thinking that more than likely he wasn't going to be summoned to Hanalei. I had a strong feeling the 'urgent family matter' had nothing to do with me or my pitiful two-person family.

***

The next morning I called the law offices of Raymond Albrecht, Esquire, and Valentine Fabares, Attorney-at-Law. I gave my name as 'Pali Moon' and asked to speak to Ms. Fabares. She came on the line almost immediately.

"Ms. Moon, I'm glad you called," she said. She did sound glad, which made me relax a little. She'd probably already realized her mistake and was as eager as I was to clear it up.

"Yes, well it seems there's been a mistake," I said.

"Oh, how so?"

"I received a letter from your office, but I'm most likely not the person you're looking for."

"Why do you say that?"

"Well, I don't have any family except a younger half-brother. I talked to him last night and he doesn't have any 'urgent matter' to discuss with me. So, I'm pretty sure the 'family matter' you referred to in your letter doesn't involve me."

She was silent for a bit before she responded.

"Ms. Moon, I can assure you with the upmost authority that you are indeed the person we're seeking. Is your birthdate June 14, 1976?"

"Yes."

"How many people with your legal name do you think were born on that date?"

I nearly snorted. Most likely there was no person born on any date in history who had the same ludicrous name as the one my parents had unloaded on me.

"So, you think I should come to the meeting?" I said.

"Yes, we definitely would appreciate your presence. Is transportation going to be a problem?"

I paused to figure out what she was getting at. "Oh, do you mean can I afford the plane ticket to get there?"

"Precisely."

"*Mahalo*, but I'm good. *Kama'aina* fares to the neighbor islands aren't that bad."

Kama'aina is what we call people who make their home in the islands. *Malihini* is what we call visitors. The distinction is carefully drawn, especially when it comes to what we're charged for everyday goods and services.

"But can you at least give me a rough idea of what this meeting is about?" I said.

"According to the wishes of my client, I really can't." She sounded downright sorry.

"Well, if I'm going to go to all the trouble of taking time off work and flying over there, don't you think I have a right to know what we're talking about here? I mean, if I'm being sued or something, I'd rather not come."

"I'm not at liberty to tell you the details of what will be discussed, but I give you my word you are not being sued. It will definitely be in your best interest to be here."

"O-kay." I dragged the word out, giving Valentine a few more seconds to reconsider and give me just a tiny hint of what this was all about.

"Excellent," she said. "Then I'll look forward to seeing you on the twenty-seventh." She didn't wait for me to say good-bye before she hung up.

I called the airline to reserve a seat on a flight to Lihue, Kaua'i. To get there in time for the meeting it was best for me to fly from Maui to Honolulu and then go on from there to Lihue. The overall distance wasn't far, but it would take me a couple of hours to get there. The reservations agent told me I'd have to go to the Kahului airport and buy the ticket in person if I wanted the *kama'aina* rate. I figured they wanted to eyeball my Hawaii ID before handing over an inter-island ticket priced at about half the tourist fare.

***

My boyfriend of one-and-a-half years, Honolulu-cop turned Maui-firefighter Hatch Decker, called me soon after I'd hung up from the airlines. I hesitated before answering because it was already ten o'clock and I was seriously late for work.

"Hey, I hope you had a good birthday," he said. "I'm real sorry I couldn't get anyone to cover my shift yesterday. We're still on for tonight, though, right?"

"Yeah, I'm looking forward to it. Are you sure your wallet can handle Mama's Fish House? It's about as spendy as it gets."

"No prob. We've got reservations at eight. But how about later today? Have you got a full schedule or can you pop down here this afternoon for a little 'party before the party'?"

"I'd love to but I've got a wedding couple coming in at eleven. Judging from my phone conversation with the bride, it's either a renewal ceremony or a late-in-life marriage. Either way, this lady seems bound and determined to get her money's worth. I'm praying I'll be able to be done with her by six."

"That's what I like about my job," Hatch said. "We get in and get out. Nobody jaws with us while their house is burning down or when we're cutting them out of a wreck. So, how about it? Should I pick you up at say, six-thirty?"

"Maybe I'll come down to your place. You're right on the way to Mama's. And besides, I'll already be down in Kahului. I've got to make a run out to the airport and pick up a ticket."

"Where're you going?"

"I've got to go to Kaua'i later this month."

"Why?"

"I got a letter from a lawyer over there. I've been invited to a meeting on the twenty-seventh. The lawyer said it's regarding an 'urgent family matter'."

"But I thought your only family was Jeff."

"It is," I said. "And I talked to Jeff and he doesn't know anything about it."

"Weird."

"Yeah, really weird. But I called the lawyer and she convinced me I'm definitely the one she wants to see."

"When's the meeting?"

"On Wednesday, the twenty-seventh. Hopefully, I'll be able to fly in and fly out the same day. Not much reason to stay over."

His end of the call went silent.

"Hatch? You still there?"

"Yeah. Hey, I'd really like to pick you up at your place. After all, it's your birthday dinner. And I'll take you to the airport before we head over to the restaurant. We'll have plenty of time."

***

The couple who showed up at my shop at eleven o'clock that morning was indeed an older couple, probably in their mid- to late-sixties. She was a half-foot shorter than I, about five feet tall, with a short cap of what looked like Clairol Nice 'n Easy Tawny Honey Blond hair. Her body had gone a bit soft around the edges but she was still in good shape. The groom was a few inches taller, with a bit of a paunch and a moon pie face that looked even moonier due to his cue-ball bald pate. His shiny noggin seemed to beg my hand to rub across it to see if it felt as smooth as it looked.

I gestured for them to each take a seat in the guest chairs across from my desk. I scurried to the other side and sat down in my creaky teak swivel chair.

I like working with older brides for a bunch of reasons. First off, unlike twenty-somethings, their wedding isn't the first grown-up thing they've ever done so they usually don't get all 'bossy pants' on me. And, they aren't hell-bent on everything being 'perfect' and falling into fits of fury if the 'dusty pink' headbands turn out to be more like 'heather pink.' And finally, I haven't met one yet who thinks she's competing with Kim Kardashian for most over-the-top wedding ever. I mean, *three* wedding dresses? After the dust settled, it turned out Kim K had more dresses than months of holy matrimony.

"I'm Mrs. Eleanor Baines," said the bride, opening up the conversation. "I've been widowed for almost five years now. And this is my new hubby-to-be, Charles Lindberg. Isn't that funny?"

After a beat of confusion I realized what she considered 'funny' was her fiancé's name. It was the same as the well-known aviator who, in 1927, made the first non-stop flight across the Atlantic Ocean.

"Oh, as you may know, Charles Lindbergh is a beloved name here on Maui, Mrs. Baines," I said. "When the original Mr. Lindbergh was alive he traveled all over the world, but Maui was his favorite place. He's buried up near Hana, you know."

"First of all, dear, please call me Eleanor. And, as you'll see on our marriage license, my Charles doesn't put the 'h' on the end of Lindberg like that other fella did. But this is also my Charles' favorite place. That's why we want to get married here."

So far, ol' Cue-ball Charlie hadn't uttered a sound. He sat there looking like a kid at the dentist while mommy did all the talking.

I nodded. "Great. Well, I'm here to make your wedding dreams come true. Let's begin by getting the paperwork out of the way." I handed them a wedding consultation form to fill out and two pens. Eleanor snapped up one of the pens and completed the entire form in record time. Charles used the opportunity to count the buttons on my shirt.

"Here you are," Eleanor said handing me back the form. "And you want a deposit of how much, dear?"

"I usually request a thousand dollars, either check or credit card. And I ask for a credit card number to keep on file. After the wedding dinner I'll present you with the total invoice, but if you want to keep it all on the same card, I'll run it the next day so you don't have to be bothered."

Eleanor plucked a Platinum American Express card from her wallet and slid it across the desk. I wrote down the information and handed it back.

"Good," she said as she tucked her wallet away. "Now that we've gotten *you* taken care of, let's see about taking care of *me*, shall we?" She dragged a thick manila file folder out of her luggage-sized purse and started flipping out photos and swatches like a blackjack dealer with a five-deck shoe. The afternoon slipped away in a torrent of questions and demands for 'must haves,' 'what do you think of's,' and 'how much for's".

When I finally got home at ten minutes after six I was starving. I grabbed a yogurt, but only ate half of it. I didn't want to spoil my appetite for the scrumptious birthday dinner I'd be enjoying at one of Maui's premiere seafood restaurants, Mama's Fish House.

I jumped in the shower. Fifteen minutes later I was wearing the only dress I owned, a short black shift with a wide band of tropical flowers circling the hem. I did a quick touch-up of the big three—blush, mascara, and lipstick. Then I rummaged through my closet searching for my one pair of sandals that weren't made of rubber.

"You look great," said Hatch when I opened the door at precisely six-thirty.

"You smell great," I said, inhaling the sweet scent of machismo—soap, Old Spice and the lingering odor of smoke that firefighters can never get out of their hair.

"We had a big one go up in Wailuku today. Did you see it on the news?"

"No, I just got home. My wedding couple turned out to be talkers. Or, to be fair, *she* was a talker. The guy she's marrying never said a word."

"It was a warehouse. Probably another insurance job." Hatch wasn't big on discussing the day-to-day challenges of my wedding business. At first I found it infuriating that I'd tell him how annoying my clients had been that day and he'd change the subject. Now I find it refreshing. No matter how stressful my day, I can always count on Hatch to get my mind off work.

"You think it was arson?" I said.

"Yeah, in this economy it's become a favorite method of unloading upside-down real estate. This is the third one this month."

"Huh. Are you sure you don't mind running me out to the airport before we go to dinner?"

"I've been thinking about that," he said. "Why don't I go to Kaua'i with you? I can add a vacation day to my usual two-days off. We could hang out and relax before you have to go to your lawyer thing. It'll be fun. Kind of like a pretend honeymoon."

I shot him my *'what the heck does that mean'*? face.

He gave me a '*no worries*' shrug.

"What do you mean 'pretend honeymoon'? I said. The shrug hadn't explained much.

"It means we'll have a great time. It also means we'll probably get our room upgraded if we tell them we're honeymooners."

We parked in the airport parking lot and walked across the street to the Hawaiian Airlines departures area. The waiting line for the ticket counter stretched through the open-air lobby and out on to the sidewalk.

"This is going to take forever," I said. I looked up at the 'Arrivals and Departures' board. "Looks like they've got a wide-body heading to the mainland in an hour."

"Stay here," said Hatch. "I'll be right back."

I watched as he bobbed and weaved through the crowd like a wide receiver sprinting downfield after shaking off an entire defensive line. I lost him in the swirl of sunburned tourists dragging bulging suitcases through the Disneyland-style check-in line.

Hatch returned less than five minutes later waving two airline tickets.

"How'd you do that?" I said.

"We did a terrorist drill with the TSA last week. I dropped a name and a ticket agent whose shift was ending offered to stay a few minutes more." He handed me my ticket. "Happy birthday, Pali."

The ticket was for the twenty-fifth, two days before my meeting on the twenty-seventh.

"I've got it all worked out," said Hatch. "If it all goes according to plan, by the time that meeting rolls you'll have forgotten what the word 'urgent' even means."

I hugged him. This birthday was turning out way better than I'd expected.

3

The best way to describe Mama's Fish House is 'heaven on earth.' Anyway, I hope heaven's got a palm grove flanking a pristine beach with blinding white sand and soft turquoise water. And I hope in heaven it'll be possible to get fish so fresh it tastes like a breeze blowing in off the ocean. And I hope the meals will be served on gorgeous square plates garnished with purple and white orchids. Maui's got dozens of five-star restaurants. Most of them are ridiculously overpriced, with lovely ambiance and creative chefs. Mama's Fish House is all of that, but with one small distinction: the setting. Mama's Fish House is in such a breathtakingly stunning location it's nearly impossible to grumble when the check comes.

While Hatch and I sipped twenty-dollar mai tais we talked about our upcoming trip to Kaua'i.

"So we're going over on the Monday before?" I said. "You know June is one of my busy months."

"It's almost the end of June. You can afford a few days off. You deserve it."

"Care to elaborate on your earlier reference to a 'pretend honeymoon'?" I said.

He ducked his head. "Hey, I was just saying we'll have fun. We both work so much it's hard to kick back and leave it behind. One thing about living here is the visitors are always having way more fun than we are. I say, let's play tourist."

"That's all?"

"That's all." He reached across the table and squeezed my hand.

I'd be lying if I said I wasn't a tiny bit disappointed. Not that I was eager to become my own client any time soon, but still it'd be nice to be asked.

From Mama's we went back to Hatch's place in Sprecklesville. He lives on a sprawling multi-million-dollar compound owned by an Australian film producer. Hatch occupies the caretaker's shack, which is no 'shack' at all. It's a modern two-bedroom, two-bath house built in the plantation style favored by old-time sugar barons and modern Hollywood-types.

Hatch's dog, Wahine, greeted us at the door in a hail of barking and leaping. She's the offspring of Farrah's dog so both dogs shared a lineage of hyper-activity and high intelligence.

"Chill it, Heen," Hatch said, using his shorthand version of her name. He scooped the dog up in his arms. "Pali doesn't want to be licked to death. At least not by you." He winked at me.

This was a side of Hatch I loved but rarely saw. Our relationship had started out kind of rocky, with misunderstandings and ambivalence on both our parts. Now he seemed to be hinting about taking it to the next level. Not that he'd admit it.

We sat outside drinking wine and not saying much for about half an hour.

"It's nice to see you in a dress," he finally said. "How come you always wear pants?"

I stared at him. "Did you really just say that?"

"Yeah. What's wrong? You have great legs. You should show them off more."

"Thank you, and duly noted. So, tell me what we're going to do in Kaua'i while we wait for my meeting?"

"Well, I thought we could do some beach stuff and eat at a couple of great restaurants. Maybe do a little hiking and sightseeing. You know, pretty much the tourist full monty."

"If we have time, I'd like to go up and see where I lived when I was a little kid," I said. "It's probably all different now, but I'd still like to see it. It's where my mom was laid to rest." I couldn't go on. My throat had closed up so tight I was having a hard time breathing, let alone talking.

"Hey, we'll go wherever you want," Hatch said. "Are you sure you'll be able to find the place? Thirty years is a long time."

"Yeah." I barely croaked it out. "I'll find it. I remember it like it was last month."

A few days after her death, my mom's friends had performed a 'return to the womb' ceremony while I watched from the beach. I remember shaking my head 'no' when someone offered to take me out on their surfboard to watch them release her ashes into the ocean. My most vivid memory was trying to comfort my little brother. He was naked like most of the kids whose parents had once lived at Taylor Camp. When the paddlers pushed off he began running down the beach screaming 'mama, mama' as if it'd finally dawned on him she was gone forever.

I'm still not exactly sure how my mom died. I'd been told she'd died of 'cerebral hemorrhage' which sounded like a stroke, but as I grew older I overheard whispered references to a drug overdose and even suicide. It isn't something I like to think about.

"Look, I want us to have fun," Hatch said. "But if it's important to you to see some stuff from your past, we can do that too. I just hope it won't bum you out. Time and tide, and all that." He squeezed my hand.

I nodded. "Oh, I forgot to tell you something. The lawyer letter was addressed to my legal name."

"But you told me hardly anybody knows your real name."

"That's right."

"You think the lawyer is going to talk about your mom?"

"What else could it be?" I said.

"Well, whatever it is, I'll be right there with you. We can handle this, Pali."

I stayed overnight at Hatch's but my mind was elsewhere. He was tender and considerate, but I picked up an undercurrent of exasperation. I didn't blame him. I was so consumed with 'what if' scenarios about my mom I was just going through the motions with Hatch.

The next morning I started lining up vendors for Eleanor and Charles' beachside wedding on the Fourth of July. I had two other weddings before I left on the twenty-fifth so I'd be busy right up until it was time to get on the plane. But busy was good. Busy meant I had no time to fret about lawyers and meetings and ugly revelations about my mom.

***

On the Friday before we were scheduled to leave for Kaua'i I went to Farrah's store.

"Hey, how's it going?" I said over the sound of the tinkly bell.

"If it was going any better, it'd be gone," she said. "You getting amped about your trip?"

"Yeah. I've been working so hard this month it'll be good to get away, but I still can't imagine what the 'urgent family matter' could be."

"Ours is not to wonder why," Farrah said. "In any case, don't get bummed about seeking the truth. The truth shall set you free, right?"

"Yeah, right. But I'm hoping the truth isn't so lousy it totally blots out any good memories I have of my mom."

"We're talking about your mother, Pali. You loved her and she loved you. No matter what happened, she was a good mom."

"What kind of a 'good mom' OD's or kills herself when she has two little kids to raise? I mean, my dad was already in the wind. She left us *orphans*. If Auntie Mana hadn't stepped up and taken us in, we'd have ended up in the system."

"I know. But don't go jumping ship before your feet are wet. Maybe you'll find out something good. Like maybe she got swept out to sea trying to rescue somebody. Or maybe she was helping sick people and she got sick, too. You know, like Father Damien."

"The whole Taylor Camp thing was pretty sick. A bunch of hippies living in tree houses smoking dope and picking up welfare checks. They weren't 'do-gooder' hippies, Farrah. They were selfish degenerates. When the State kicked them off the beach they just went and squatted somewhere else."

"Even so. We're talking about your *ohana*. And as screwed up as family can be, it's still family."

Only Farrah could make the absurd sound almost rational.

I told her I wouldn't be coming in to my shop over the weekend. "I have a wedding in Kapalua tomorrow and then another one at Napili on Sunday. Our plane leaves early Monday morning."

"Well, have a great time with Hatch," said Farrah. "And don't worry about that meeting at the lawyer's. Whatever it is—it is, right? When are you coming home?"

"After the meeting. I think the flight's at five o'clock."

"Give me a shout when you're back, okay?"

A customer came in and Farrah leaned in and gave me a quick hug. I darted out the back. No matter what happened in Kaua'i, I knew my true *ohana* was right there on Maui.

4

On Monday morning the plane left bright and early. We flew into Honolulu and then caught a flight to Lihue. We arrived in Kaua'i at eight in the morning. Most of our fellow passengers spent the short flight pecking away on computers so I figured the first flight of the day must cater to people going over on business. When we landed, Hatch and I exchanged a glance before racing across the street to the rental car building. Everything moves slow on the neighbor islands, including the rental car lines.

"Who'd you book the car from?" I said as we sprinted down the row of rental car kiosks.

"Oh man. I knew there was something I forgot."

We screeched to a halt. I looked around and noticed chickens in the airport parking lot.

"Look," I said. "Someone's chickens escaped."

We started at the first counter and worked our way down asking each clerk if they had any cars available and if they offered *kama'aina* rates. We ended up with a nondescript white Nissan Altima. Hatch got a discount because he was a local firefighter. My Auntie Mana used to say, '*You don't ask, you don't get.*' Locals are never shy about asking for deals and special favors. It's as much an island tradition as shooting the thumb and pinkie *shaka* sign instead of waving.

"It's too early to check into our room," said Hatch. "You want to do some sightseeing?"

"Sounds good to me."

"Since we're staying in Poipu let's check out the West Side. If we get back to the hotel around three they should have the room ready."

We headed west on Highway 50 toward Waimea Canyon, but Hatch first wanted to stop and see the 'Spouting Horn' in Lawa'i Bay. We knew we were at the right place when we saw three tour busses lined up in the parking lot. We got out and there were chickens pecking in the grass strip next to the lot.

"What's with the chickens?" Hatch said.

I shook my head. "No clue. Chickens running around like this on Maui would be *teriyaki* by now."

The locals had fashioned a make-shift craft fair with a gauntlet of tarp-covered tables on the path to view the sight. At first I looked away as I marched past table after table of hand-made jewelry and cheesy souvenirs, but about halfway down something caught my eye. It was a glass Christmas ornament decorated with a glittery sun, moon, and stars. Three cut crystals had been tied on the hanging string about an inch apart. A shaft of light hit the crystals creating a scattering of tiny rainbows on the ground. It looked handmade, but it was tough to tell if it had been made locally or in a sweatshop in China.

"I'll bet Farrah would love this," I said.

"It's pretty. But what is it?"

"It's a Christmas ornament."

"But it's June. Christmas is six months away."

As a firefighter, Hatch lives almost exclusively in the present. The bell sounds and off they go. They don't plan ahead, they react when needed. Although they're constantly training so they'll be effective when the call comes, their everyday work life is pretty much dictated moment to moment.

"Believe me, she'll love it. She'll hang it in her window until it's time to put up her Christmas tree."

I bought the ornament and we continued toward the fenced shoreline.

The "Spouting Horn" is a blowhole in a lava tube formed when volcanoes were still erupting on Kaua'i. The tube runs all the way to the ocean. Every few minutes the waves force water and air through a shelf in the tube and create an upward spray of water that looks like a geyser. A posted sign describing the site said water can shoot as high as fifty feet, but it looked like only half that high to me.

What got my attention was the weird moaning and sighing sounds coming from the blowhole.

"You hear that?" said Hatch. "Sounds kinda sexy."

I gave him a playful dig to the ribs. "How does your mind work? You probably think a *tsunami* siren sounds sexy."

A perky tour guide waving a yellow plastic flower on the end of a stick motioned to a cluster of tourists. They trotted over to where we were standing.

"This blowhole is one example of the ingenuity of the ancient Hawaiians to make sense of their world," she said. "The early inhabitants lost many people to the undertow in this area. They figured this stretch of coastline along Lawa'i Bay must be guarded by a giant *mo'o* or lizard. The belief was that anyone who came down here to fish or swim would get killed by the *mo'o* and so they stayed away. One day a man named Liko bravely went into the bay. It didn't take long for the *mo'o* to spot him and go after him. But Liko was quick. He swam to the lava tube and popped to the surface through a hole in the roof of the tube. The giant *mo'o* followed but got stuck because the hole was too small for the enormous lizard to get through. The sounds you hear are the groans of the trapped *mo'o*. See his steamy breath spraying from the hole? He's still there, wrestling to free himself from his agonizing fate."

"Still think it sounds sexy?" I whispered to Hatch.

"Maybe it does to an enormous *girl* lizard," he said with a wink.

After the Spouting Horn we doubled back and made our way to Highway 530 and then on to Highway 50, the main south-to-west road on Kaua'i.

We approached the town of Waimea. Waimea is a funky little town that reminded me of Pa'ia back home. It has a stately columned bank, but the rest of the town is mostly aging wooden buildings that appear to have seen their share of termites. As we drove through town I noticed a bright yellow clapboard building with "Toto's Shave Ice" painted on the side. In case there was any question of what they were selling, there was also a five-foot high wooden tent with a painted rainbow shave ice cone on each side.

"I love shave ice," said Hatch. "Let's get some after I check out this front tire. The light's been on since we picked up the car and I don't want a flat in the middle of nowhere."

We pulled into a gas station. Hatch got out and went to find someone with a tire gauge. I got out to stretch my legs. Hatch returned and a few minutes later a guy came out wiping his hands on a purple rag.

"You got a problem with the tire?" he said. A patch on his shirt said, *Keoni*.

"Yeah," Hatch said, pointing to the offending tire. "Can I use your gauge?"

"No problem, man. I do it."

Hatch beat the guy to the ground in an attempt to unscrew the valve stem cap before Keoni could get there.

"Man, it's cool," said Keoni in a somewhat offended tone. "I do stuff like this all day."

Hatch stood by looking uncomfortable with another man doing 'man things' for him.

"You need a little air. I'll fill it."

Keoni pulled the air hose out and began filling the tire. When he finished, Hatch nodded toward the yellow building across the street. "Is that Toto's Shave Ice any good?" he said.

Keoni stood up "We got two Toto's, ya know. Old one and new one.".

"Two? They must be doing good to have two."

"Nah. Totally different people own 'em."

"But how can they have the same name?"

"Okay, so way back when, this girl Toto starts up a shave ice shop when she gets outta high school. She gets herself a special ice shaver that makes the ice real soft, almost like snow, eh? Everybody love it. They put her place in the tourist books and lots of people come here for the best shave ice on the whole island. Maybe the best anywhere."

Hatch nodded.

The guy pointed to our windshield. "You want I clean your window for you?"

"Nah, that's okay. It's a rental. We live on Maui. We just came over for a visit."

"You want I give you good price on a map?"

"*Mahalo*, but we don't need a map," said Hatch. "Kaua'i is pretty easy. Pretty much one big loop."

"True dat," said the guy. "So anyways, after a few years Toto decides she wants to go to college. You know, to get her education. So she sells the shave ice store and goes off to be a teacher. When she comes back she starts teaching at the high school. But things are tough over here, ya know? The kids can't get jobs or nothin' and they fall into bad ways. Like drugs and all that. So she figure if she starts up another shave ice it will give the high school kids someplace to work and make money. She calls the new place Toto's *Anuenue* Shave Ice." He grinned. "Get it?"

Hatch looked confused. "Not really."

"It's like a joke, man. *Anuenue* is the Hawaiian word for 'rainbow' but it also sounds like 'new-new" in English. So everybody call tell which Toto's is which. She one smart girl, that Auntie Toto."

"Which one do you recommend?" I chimed in.

"They both good, but I mostly go to Toto's *Anuenue* because she got the school kids working there and she got all the flavors I like. Lots of 'em."

"Where's Toto's *Anuenue*?"

"Down there by the bank." He pointed to the stately columned building we'd driven past on our way into town. "It's right across. You can't miss it."

"*Mahalo*," I said.

"Hey, Keoni, can I ask one more thing?" said Hatch. "What's with the chickens everywhere?"

"Those chickens?" Keoni pointed to a couple of hens and a brightly-colored rooster pecking in the weeds.

"Yeah," said Hatch. "Everywhere we go on this island we see wild chickens."

"Kaua'i is known for the *moa*, man. They come from fighting stock. When Hurricane Iniki ripped the island apart in 1992, everything got leveled. Lots of guys who raised fighting cocks had their cages blown away and the birds got loose. But those birds are tough; they survived. Now we got *moa* everywhere."

"But they're chickens," Hatch said. "Why didn't they end up on somebody's hibachi?"

"Oh, some people tried. No good. Like I say, man, those chickens are *tough*. And they got worms and stuff. Nobody around here eats those buggahs."

Hatch pulled a few dollar bills from his wallet but Keoni waved it off. "My pleasure, bro. Bes' thing you can do for me is give a good tip to those kids working down at the shave ice."

We thanked him and drove down to Toto's Anuenue. Sure enough, there were two high-school age girls working at the shop. One was at the counter and the other was operating the ice machine.

"*Aloha*," said the counter girl as we pulled the door closed behind us. "Welcome to Toto's. What can I get for you today?"

I looked at the menu board. The gas station guy was right. Auntie Toto had every possible flavor of shave ice. Some were stand-bys, like papaya, blue raspberry and cherry. But some were pretty off-the-wall, like cotton candy and butterscotch.

"How many flavors have you got?" said Hatch.

"About fifty. But most people get 'rainbow'," said the girl. "I can make a shave ice rainbow with any flavors you want. Go ahead and pick. But first, do you want ice cream or azuki bean at the bottom?"

The shave ice machine was whirring away in the background.

"Azuki bean," I said. "I haven't had that in years."

Hatch ordered two rainbows, one with beans and one with macadamia nut ice cream. We took our treats outside and sat on a narrow wooden bench in front. Waimea bustled around us. We watched people going to the bank, trucks delivering boxes to the liquor store next door, and mothers pushing strollers in the park across the street. And chickens. At least a dozen chickens pecked in the shade of the towering trees in the park.

"You know," I said. "We're eating dessert and we haven't even had lunch yet," I said.

"I thought this *was* lunch," said Hatch shoveling shave ice into his mouth with a red-striped plastic straw-spoon. "Back in LA we had snow cones at the beach but these are better."

"That's because Hawaii shave ice is different. The ice is shaved rather than just crushed. The syrup sticks to it better. You know, Hawaiian shave ice actually originated in Japan a thousand years ago," I said. "The Japanese cane workers brought the idea of shave ice to the islands back in the late 1800's."

"Where'd they get the ice?" said Hatch. "It's not like they had freezers."

"They carried large blocks of ice in the holds of sailing ships. According to Japanese legend, they shaved the ice with ceremonial swords."

We finished up and got back on the road. We were headed up to Waimea Canyon—the Grand Canyon of the Pacific—and we still had to make it up the twisty two-lane road that goes to the top.

When we got to the canyon, the obligatory tour busses had taken up most of the parking lot. The overlooks were jammed with Japanese tourists. It seemed everyone was either taking a photo or posing for a photo. Tour guides chattered and gestured to the crowds like auctioneers.

After a few minutes the busses honked their horns and the tourists hustled back to the parking lot. With a belch of exhaust the caravan of busses roared away leaving us alone. The wind whistled eerily through the canyon and tossed Hatch's hair across his forehead.

I pulled out my phone to take his picture. "Say 'azuki bean'," I said and snapped the photo.

***

At four o'clock we finally pulled into the resort Hatch had booked for our two-night stay. I looked over and shot him an '*are you serious*?' grin. The place was way more la-di-dah than I was expecting.

The open-air lobby had thirty-foot ceilings and marble floors. Across from the entrance were four immense pillars. Beyond the pillars was a spectacular view of sweeping lawns, golden sand, and waves crashing on the nearby shoreline. On the right side of the lobby a sumptuous bar, complete with koi pond, potted palms and dark rattan furniture beckoned with promises of umbrella drinks in hollowed-out pineapples. A poster showed a smiley local guy posing with his *ukulele*, announcing live music every night after six p.m.

Our room was equally posh. It was a two-bedroom, two-bath suite with living room, dining room and full kitchen. The master bedroom had a four-poster king bed draped in yards of dramatic mosquito netting, and the second bedroom had a queen bed with a mattress so far off the ground it had a matching step-stool alongside.

"Are you expecting guests?" I said.

Hatch smiled. "No, but this was the last ocean view room available. And what the heck, we might want to try out all the beds. You know, like Little Red Riding Hood and the Three Bears."

"I think it was Goldilocks who went from bed to bed," I said.

"Hmm, sounds about right. Blonds are known for being bed-hoppers."

I'm a few shades down from blond but on behalf of blonds everywhere I shot him some *stink eye*.

"Now don't get all worked up over this place having a kitchen," Hatch said. "I'm not expecting you to cook."

"Well, I wouldn't mind making breakfast," I said. "Look at that view."

The spacious balcony *lanai* overlooked a wide vista of sapphire ocean blending into an expanse of blinding cobalt sky. The patio furniture included a small teak table with two heavy teak armchairs. There was also a matching lounge with comfy four-inch-thick cushion.

"I sometimes forget how calming the ocean can be," I said. Back home I live in upcountry Maui, far from the beach. The upside of upcountry is it has few tourists, little traffic, and lower housing prices. The downside is there's no ocean sound, no turtles bobbing their heads up for a peek and no briny smell of fresh air that's been scrubbed clean after crossing thousands of miles of water.

In the living room the suite had been done up with the expected resort décor: sepia-toned etchings of hula dancers, a floor lamp that looked like a miniature palm tree, and thick blond bamboo furniture with Hawaiian print cushions. If Hatch wanted to play tourist for a couple of days he'd certainly picked the right place to do it. And I was happily tagging along. After all, even though I'd been born in Kaua'i, it was no longer home. I was a visitor. And I was going to take advantage of all the perks that visitors take for granted. For the next couple of days I was going to eat whatever I wanted, drink more adult beverages than I should, and lie around until my body begged to be vertical.

"The website said this place has a two million-dollar workout facility," Hatch said. "Want to go check it out?"

"Not hardly."

While Hatch went to do his body good, I plopped down on the *lanai* to catch a few rays. I had two more days to relax before the lawyer meeting in Hanalei. For all I knew, this might be my last few days of idyllic ignorance. On Wednesday I'd be forced to abandon my gauzy made-up family history and embrace the prickly truth about who I was. Worse, I'd have to face the ugly truth about why my mother just had up and died at the tender age of twenty-five.

5

When I awoke Tuesday morning, Hatch was already in the kitchen. I tip-toed toward the bathroom to make myself presentable, but he stepped in front of me before I got there.

"Two sugars, extra creamer," he said handing me a cup of coffee.

"*Mahalo*," I said. I could only imagine what I looked like after the three *mai tais* I'd sucked down at dinner the night before, but Hatch seemed to take my disheveled appearance in stride.

We sat on the sofa and sipped our coffee. The coffee table was littered with stacks of tourist information Hatch had picked up from a display in the lobby. He picked up a handful of brochures and fanned them out in front of me.

"How about a helicopter ride?" he said. "You ever been up in a chopper?"

I didn't want to let on I'd gone on my first helicopter ride six months earlier with Ono Kingston, a friend of mine who'd made it clear he'd like to take our relationship to the next level.

"I bet this island's gorgeous from the air," I said, avoiding the question.

"Yeah. This is the perfect place for helicopters," Hatch said. "Lots of inaccessible cliffs and tons of great waterfalls. You don't think you'll get airsick or anything, right?"

I screwed up my face. "Airsick? Are you serious?" Hatch knew I'd worked as a federal air marshal after college. In air marshal training they'd thrown everything they had at us to make us get sick, disoriented or scared. I passed without a whimper. No way I'd give them the satisfaction. I still say they pushed the female recruits twice as hard as the guys.

"Great," he said. "Which company do you want to go with?" He plucked out three brochures.

I put down my coffee mug. "Let's take this one, Safari Helicopters," I said. "They say they have the smoothest ride. I'll be fine, but I don't want you tossing your plate lunch if we hit a downdraft."

An hour later we pulled up at the helicopter tour office. The tour began with an entertaining FAA briefing about wearing the life preserver, how to enter and exit the aircraft and what to expect on the ride. I think 'entertaining' was the operative word, since it seemed they'd learned if you want people to pay attention to the safety information you need to present it in an amusing way.

"Okay guys and gals," said the briefing guy. "The ride you're about to go on is all about color. We got green in the valleys and our beautiful blue sky and ocean. We even got pink, red and brown up in Waimea Canyon. But in the unlikely event of a water landing, do you know what your favorite color will be?" He reached down and picked up a bright yellow pouch the size of a hardback book. "That's right, people—sunshine yellow!" He demonstrated how to don the vest over your head and clip on the waist belt. "Now for those who are worried about packing on a few inches on vacation, take heart. You'll be wearing this baby around your waist for the entire flight today. When the ride's over and you take it off you're gonna feel so skinny you'll feel like ordering *both* the mac salad and rice with your lunch."

The briefing went on like that for about ten minutes. Then we trooped out to the van and the guy drove us to a helipad at the edge of the Lihue airport tarmac. I looked up and hoped the helicopter pilot was as mindful of the planes swooping by overhead as I was.

The briefing guy gave us each a number so we could be seated according to weight. Back at the tour office a potential female passenger who my Auntie Mana would've described as an '*ali'i*-sized girl' had expressed dismay at being asked to step on a scale.

"No worries," said the equally *ali'i*-sized gal working behind the desk. "See? There's no numbers on the scale."

She was right. The read-out was discretely positioned so only the gal behind the desk could see how much each person weighed. She'd assigned the seats accordingly and now we were taking our positions alongside the helicopter.

I got number five and Hatch was six. I figured that meant we'd be in the back since the helicopter only held six passengers. But as they loaded everyone in, it soon became clear we'd be sitting in front. I was positioned next to the pilot. The large bubble window gave me a perfect one-eighty view.

"Welcome aboard," the pilot said as we got in and put on our headsets. I slipped into my shoulder harness and clipped on my seat belt.

"Hey," I said. "Good to be here." But then I realized no one could hear me. Only the pilot had a mic on his headset. The passenger voices were lost in the *whoosh, whoosh, whoosh* of the slowly turning rotors.

When the bird lifted off, I remembered how effortless flying in a helicopter felt. The pilot said it would feel like riding a magic carpet. I thought that sounded a little too cute, but kept it to myself. He said if we had questions to use the handheld mics in front of us. There was one in the front and one in the back. We flew up and over the resorts of Poipu. The pilot asked each couple where they were staying and he pointed out each resort from the air.

We flew into brilliant green canyons cut deep with sheer cliffs on all sides. As we shot up the cliff sides to get into the next canyon I found myself lifting my toes to help the helicopter clear the treetops.

Waterfalls and rainbows popped into view as we glided in and out of the canyons. Even though I'd scoffed at the pilot's 'magic carpet' remark, I was starting to agree.

We approached the North Shore and I peered down at the beach bordered by deep green jungle and tried to find a recognizable landmark. I picked up the handheld mic and pushed the 'talk' button.

"Have you ever heard of Taylor Camp?" I said.

"Sure," said the pilot. "It's pretty much gone now, but back in the seventies a bunch of hippies lived up there. They built amazing tree houses. The guy who owned the land, Howard Taylor, was the brother of actress Elizabeth Taylor."

"Isn't it around here somewhere?" I said into the mic.

"Yep, hold on."

He pulled the joystick back and left and the helicopter wheeled into a tight turn. Even with my headset on and the rotors roaring I could hear the people in the back go, "Whoa" as my stomach lurched with the turn.

"It's right down there. Do you see that stretch of sand? That's Ke'e Beach Park. Taylor's Camp was around there somewhere. I think if you want to see it, the trail's still visible. But I'm not sure. I've never been up there."

We swooped over a cluster of buildings and homes set along a wide bay. "That's the little town of Hanalei down there," said the pilot. "Anybody know what Hanalei's known for?"

I let someone else get credit for knowing about "Puff the Magic Dragon."

The pilot nodded. "Yeah, that's from the old days. How about more recently? Did anyone see the movie, 'The Descendants'? Hanalei is where George Clooney tracked down the guy who was having an affair with his wife."

The large-size woman in the back picked up the mic. When she got it to work she said, "That woman should get her eyes checked. You'd have to be blind to cheat on George Clooney."

We flew straight toward a thin ribbon of waterfall streaming down thousands of feet from a dark green cleft in the side of Mount Wai'ale'ale. As we headed deeper and deeper into the canyon the pilot said, "Mount Wai'ale'ale is one of the wettest spots on earth. Its reported rainfall is over four hundred inches a year." At the last possible moment he nimbly turned the chopper around and headed back out and I allowed myself to exhale.

We left the mountains and skimmed over flat green fields on our way back to the airport. The pilot said, "Anyone want to guess how fast we're going?"

I looked at the gauges and saw one labeled "KIAS." In airspeed the value is measured in knots per hour, not miles per hour. In air marshal training we'd been given a rudimentary flying lesson. They'd told us they never expected us to fly a jumbo jet or anything, but they wanted us to at least be able to communicate with air traffic control. I took the lesson seriously. It wasn't that hard for me to imagine I might be asked to land a plane someday.

"Eighty miles an hour?" said a guy in the back.

"Nope," said the pilot. He looked over at me. "How about you? Care to take a guess?"

I flicked on the mic and checked the speedometer again. "Well, it reads one-hundred thirty knots indicated airspeed. So, that would be about a hundred and fifty miles per hour."

"You're pretty good," he said giving me a big smile. "Are you a pilot?"

Hatch tapped me on the shoulder and gestured for me to hand him the mic. "No," he said. "She's not a pilot; she's a wedding planner. She's used to answering dumb-ass questions."

The pilot shot a look at Hatch. Then he squinted in concentration and dropped the bird dead-center on the landing pad.

***

"Whew. That was great," I said after Hatch and I had gotten far enough away from the rotor wash that we could hear each other.

"Glad you liked it. Now let's see how much of this island we can cover from ground level."

We stopped in a few of the funkier shops in Kapa'a and then drove up to Kilauea. At the lighthouse overlook we peered through the binoculars and saw albatrosses and red-footed boobies on the massive rock cliffs. On our way back to the highway, we turned in at the historic Kong Lung shopping center and Hatch bought me a gorgeous silk-screened kimono with flamingo-pink lotus flowers.

"I think we should drive up to Hanalei so you can check out where you'll be going tomorrow morning," said Hatch.

I agreed, but as we descended into the Hanalei Valley from cliffs of Princeville I felt my heart rate increase and my fingers turn to ice. At the one-lane bridge on the outskirts of Hanalei we had to stop for road construction.

"You okay?" said Hatch, reaching over to take my hand. "You've been awful quiet. You know I'm willing to come with you tomorrow if you want. I can poke around town while you're at the lawyer's."

"*Mahalo*, but I'll be fine."

We crossed the bridge and made our way into town. By the time we found the address of the attorney's office, my stomach was roiling.

"You want to stop and check it out?" Hatch said as we slowly drove past the brown two-story building.

"No, thanks. But I sure wish that lawyer would've told me what this was about. Being back here brings up a lot of stuff I'd rather not think about. I remember thinking if I could hold my breath long enough, I could die and go be with my mother. A suicidal five-year-old. How sick is that?"

"It's not sick," said Hatch. "You were a little kid. Little kids need their moms."

Hatch pulled into a parking spot at the Ching Young Center. "Hey," he said. "You want to look around or have you had enough?"

"I had enough of this place thirty years ago." Where had that come from? As soon as it was out of my mouth I felt like I'd disrespected my mother's memory. "I didn't mean that. What I meant was…" I stopped, unsure of what to say next.

"Hey, no worries," he said. "Let's head back to Poipu. You'll be back here soon enough."

I nodded.

***

That night as we got ready for bed, Hatch leaned over and kissed me. "It's been great hanging out with you," he said. "I, uh…" He didn't go on.

"Are you okay?" I said.

"Yeah, I just like being here with you, that's all."

We got into bed and, as usual, he was his loving, tender self. But I could tell something was on his mind. I had my own stuff rattling around my head, but I'd promised myself I wouldn't allow it to take over. Farrah would've been pleased I'd finally taken her advice about 'staying in the present.' Distracted or not, Hatch and I both managed to 'stay in the present' for more than an hour.

6

Wednesday dawned overcast and cool for an end-of-June day. If I'd been working I'd probably be trying to convince a tearful bride that rain on her wedding day meant good luck in the marriage. I don't have any evidence it's true, but I've used that line more times than I can count since island showers occur much more frequently than the Hawaii Tourist Bureau will own up to.

Hatch got up and made coffee. While I was finishing my shower he brought a cup into the bathroom. I wrapped a towel around my head and put on my new lotus flower kimono which I'd already dubbed my 'lucky kimono.' Without a word he took me in his arms and I nuzzled into his chest. All I could hear was the drip, drip, drip of the shower and his strong slow heartbeat.

"You gonna be okay today?" he finally said.

"Yeah. I'm good. How about you? What are you going to do while I'm gone?"

"I called the fire station up the road and they've got a softball game against some off-duty cops from Lihue. They said they'd loan me a glove if I wanted to play."

"Will you be finished in time to make our flight at five?"

"It starts at ten-thirty so even if it goes to extra innings we should be done by one. Then we'll probably grab some pizza. Worst case, I'll be back here by three."

I bit the side of my lip.

"I know, it's not fair," he said. "Me playing while you suffer. But the offer's still open if you want me to go up there with you."

"*Mahalo*, but I'll be fine."

While I got dressed Hatch made breakfast. Fresh papaya with lime, scrambled eggs and Hawaiian sweet bread toast and guava jelly.

I pushed the eggs around on my plate for awhile but couldn't bring myself to actually take a bite.

"You really ought to eat something," he said placing the plate of toast in front of me. His own once full plate was now nearly empty.

"I know, but I'm so nervous."

"That's why you need to eat something. Nothing worse than bad news on an empty stomach."

I forced down a few bites of toast and then checked my watch. It was nearly eight-thirty.

"I should get going," I said. "The meeting starts at eleven."

"That's two and a half hours from now. It doesn't take more than an hour and a half to get to Hanalei."

"But there could be traffic."

He laughed. "On Kaua'i?"

"Remember that construction at the Hanalei Bridge?"

"All right. You're probably better off driving than sitting here stewing. Call me when you get there."

I promised to call and then leaned in for another long hug. "I'm sorry to be acting like such a baby," I said. "I'll make it up to you."

"Good. I'm counting on it." He gave me a quick kiss.

I went out to the car and had to shoo a chicken away so I could back out of the parking spot. I drove out of the resort and made my way to Highway 520. The highway goes through a tunnel of eucalyptus trees on the way to Lihue. In the cool green of the tree tunnel I began imagining how good it would feel to just drive wherever the road took me and forget about going to the lawyer's office. If I made a left once I passed Lihue I could go up and see Wailua Falls. Or I could head south and visit the harbor at Nawiliwili. The cruise ships come in at Nawiliwili so there would probably be shops and restaurants I could poke around in while I bided my time pretending to be at the meeting. I'd tell Hatch the meeting had been uneventful and that Valentine Fabares hadn't told me anything new.

But as I continued past the turnoff to Nawiliwili and then past the road to Wailua Falls, I knew I wouldn't be playing hooky after all. As Farrah had wisely observed, "The truth shall set you free." I guess I wanted freedom from the nagging questions about my mom more than I was willing to admit.

***

I arrived in Hanalei a few minutes after ten. It was too early to show up at the lawyer's office so I found a parking spot and sat in the car. I put in a call to Hatch but he must've already left for his game because I had to leave a voicemail. I did some deep breathing exercises I'd learned in martial arts to take my mind off agonizing over the meeting ahead but it was useless. Had my mom been so selfish she hadn't given a diddly-damn about me or my brother and had taken her own life? Or had she chosen feeding her drug habit over feeding her kids? What if I learned she'd died from a gruesome genetic condition that I'd probably inherited?

As I sat there dreaming up morbid scenarios, I felt the weight of not knowing gnawing on me like an insect burrowing underneath my skin. I became desperate to find out what happened. I got out of the car and took the stairs two at a time. The sign on the door said, "R. Albrecht and Associates, Attorneys-at-Law." No mention of 'esquire'. Looked like the associates had overruled Albrecht on the signage but he'd refused to budge on the letterhead.

I went inside and a smiling receptionist looked up from pecking on her computer.

"*Aloha.* May I help you?" she said. Her teeth were blindingly white. In order for me to get teeth that white I'd have to give up coffee for the rest of my life. Nice teeth, but no dice.

"*Aloha.* My name is Pali Moon and I'm here for an appointment with Valentine Fabares at eleven."

"Certainly. Please have a seat in our waiting room. Would you like coffee or tea?" She started to get up, but I declined anything to drink.

"Then go on in. Most of the other family members are already here."

Family members? What family members?

I went through a doorway into the small waiting room. Chairs were positioned around the walls. Four women were waiting; none seated next to the other. In the far corner a pimply-faced teen-aged boy muttered into a cell phone.

I sat in the only remaining chair that wasn't next to someone. I tried to discreetly check out the other women, but they were busy checking me out so eye contact became awkward. I picked up a magazine from a stack on a low table in the middle of the room. It turned out to be a months-old copy of *People* with a cover photo showing a smiling Sandra Bullock and her bad boy ex-husband, Jesse James. In my business I'd seen plenty of goody-goody women desperately in love with guys they thought they could 'make over.' By the time the couple showed up at my door, the guys had been house broken enough to agree to the concept of marriage—most notably the benefits of having someone to do their cooking and cleaning and the promise of sex every night—but it was easy to spot the guys who'd already mentally deleted the vow about "forsaking all others" before they'd even taken it.

I flipped through the magazine, not focusing on either pictures or words. Instead I used it as a blind to peek over while I scoped out my so-called 'family' members. Who were these people? None of them looked even vaguely familiar nor could I detect any family resemblance. Did my mother have step-sisters? Maybe cousins?

By the time eleven o'clock rolled around the tiny waiting room held six women, including me, and the one sullen teen-age boy.

A door on the other side of the room opened and a woman stepped into the doorway. She was definitely someone Farrah—or probably my hippie mother—could relate to. She had waist-length brown hair, parted in the middle. The hair looked a bit oily; like it got washed once a week and this was day six. The woman wore a long orange Indian-print cotton wrap skirt and a plain white scooped-neck tee. I looked down and expected to see worn *rubba slippas* on her feet but instead she wore bright yellow Crocs; those clunky molded-plastic shoes that look like something Minnie Mouse would wear on a date with Mickey. But unlike Farrah, the woman standing in the doorway wasn't curvy. In fact, she looked like she hadn't eaten a decent meal in weeks.

"*Aloha.* And *mahalo* to everyone for being so prompt." Her wide smile pulled her cheeks taut against well-defined cheekbones. "Let's move into the conference room, shall we?"

The teenager stayed put while the rest of us trooped down a short hall. We entered a room with an oval wooden table with eight chairs around it. On one wall, a wide window faced the mountain dubbed "Bali Hai" in the old movie, *South Pacific.* In the far corner sat a small flat-screen television on a rolling cart.

While everyone found seats around the table I gawked out the window. By the time I turned to take a seat the only chair available was the one at Croc-woman's left. I sat down. As we settled in, a guy in more-or-less professional attire—starched beige cotton aloha shirt, tan slacks and brown leather loafers—came in. He closed the door and stood in front of it with his arms crossed like a bank guard trying to look official.

"Again, *aloha*, and *mahalo* for your presence here today," said Croc-woman. She smiled at the guy standing by the door and he gave her an 'atta-girl' nod of the head. "Please accept my special *mahalo* to those of you who took time off from work and traveled to be here today." From the looks of things she was talking to me. The other women looked like they'd taken time off from retail therapy at Honolulu's Ala Moana Shopping Center and then a fifty-dollar girls' lunch at the Royal Hawaiian.

"My name is Valentine Fabares. My surname is French so it's pronounced, 'Fah-bray,' but I'm born and raised here on Kaua'i. I'm the attorney of record for the estate. I'm joined here this morning by my colleague, Tim Abbott, the CPA who assisted me with the financial reports." The guy by the door raised his hand as if the teacher was taking roll.

"Is this everyone?" said one of the women at the table. She had a prominent mole at the side of her upper lip and it was hard not to fix on it. Also, she looked older than the others by at least a decade. But it was hard to judge ages. As I scanned the group I guessed there'd been a fair amount of nipping and tucking, not to mention Botox. The lip mole woman went on, "I mean, are there others who aren't here today?"

"Just one," said Valentine. "But besides her, the people sitting at this table constitute the entire group representing the named heirs. There may be unnamed heirs who come forward later as a result of public notification, but I doubt it. But please, let's agree to hold all questions until after the reading of the will, shall we?"

Reading of the will? My mom had a will? Why had it taken thirty years to unearth her will? And why isn't my brother here?

"Let's begin." Valentine Fabares cleared her throat and began reading the last will and testament of one Phillip James Wilkerson, the Third. The will started off stating his birthdate, place of employment and addresses of various homes he claimed to own. The guy must've been loaded. He had three homes on various islands in Hawaii, two on the mainland, and an apartment in Portofino, Italy. Then Valentine read a line that stopped me cold, "I have used other names during the course of my lifetime, including the names Jim Wilkes and Coyote Moon."

I sucked in a breath. For a few moments I held it in. It was as if a cog in my brain had frozen up and shut the whole thing down. I had to consciously remind myself to do stuff that was usually automatic, like breathing and blinking.

So, this meeting wasn't about my mother or how she died. This meeting was about my *father*, Phillip James Wilkerson, the Third. He'd taken off when I was just a baby, but not before claiming me as his child. I'd often pondered my parents' names on my birth certificate and wondered if they were fake. My mother's name was listed as Martha Warner. The name typed on the 'father' line was Coyote P. Moon, of Hanalei, Hawaii.

7

Valentine Fabares kept on reading, but for the next few minutes I didn't take in much of what she said. I was otherwise occupied, listening to a seashell-like rush of sound that blotted out the world around me. I'd long ago given up any hope of finding my father so being invited to the reading of his will was about as shocking as being fingered for a crime I hadn't committed.

"…and my fourth wife was Linda Gardner Wilkerson, by whom I had two children, Kali Elizabeth Wilkerson and Nathaniel Robert Wilkerson. Their last known address was 2025 Apu'a'a Street in Honolulu, Hawaii. The children's social security numbers are…" At that point, I tuned out again. How had Wilkerson gotten everyone's addresses and social security numbers? Had Valentine already read my address and social security number? How had I missed that?

She went on reading, "My sixth wife was Susanne Marie Beatty Wilkerson. This union produced no known children. Her last known address was…"

I looked up at a clock on the wall. Valentine had been reading for more than five minutes. She ended with, "This is my last will and testament, hereby sworn to and witnessed on this day, Thursday, the fifth of August, 2010."

The room was hushed. The youngest-looking of my father's former spouses dabbed at her eyes with a tissue. Two others looked as if they were dying to dig out their smart phones and update their Facebook status. The blousy blond sitting next to me glared as if daring anyone to say a good word about the deceased.

"So that's it?" said Lip Mole Woman. "What about the money? And if Phil had six wives and one of them isn't here, why are there seven women, including you of course, sitting at this table?"

It seemed to take a couple of the gals longer than necessary to do the math.

"I'll take your last question first," said Valentine. Her voice sounded like she'd gone to the same Homeland Security hostage negotiation class I had. We'd been taught a voice tone referred to as 'CLC'—calm, low, and clear. We did a series of role plays learning to speak as if we were discussing the weather when we knew perfectly well the guy we were talking to had a loaded gun shoved to the temple of a terrified hostage. My negotiator voice had come in handy more than a few times in dealing with overwrought brides. A blue ink spot on the bodice of a four-thousand dollar wedding gown? Use the CLC voice to talk her down off the ledge. Or how about dealing with a trophy-wife stepmother showing up in the same dress, three sizes smaller, as the mother-of-the-bride? Again, go with the CLC voice to review the options.

Valentine smiled as she looked around the table and then she nodded to the guy standing by the door.

"Pardon me. I was remiss in not asking everyone to introduce themselves. Shall we do that now? I think after all the introductions are made, you'll see why we have six people here this morning instead of five."

Valentine gestured for the woman on her right to begin. I pulled out a little notebook and pen I keep in my purse. I had a feeling I may need to remember who was who later on. The first woman said her name was Linda Gardner, formerly Linda Wilkerson, and she'd been Phil's fourth wife.

The lip mole woman introduced herself as Phil's first wife, Margaret Chesterton. She said she went by 'Peggy' and she was the mother of Phil's two oldest children. She said her father had been chief of police for the Kaua'i Police Department before becoming the mayor in 1982. She went on to say she'd known Valentine Fabares for years, even decades.

"I remember when you first passed the bar exam," she said. "Daddy introduced you at a Chamber of Commerce event and you inadvertently referred to him as 'Chief Chesterton' instead of 'Mister Mayor'." She shot Valentine a smug smile that wasn't returned.

Next to her was the young blond who'd dabbed at her eyes during the reading of the will. She looked to be my age, maybe even a little younger. When she spoke, her voice was low and breathy. She said her name was Susanne Wilkerson, but she liked to be called Sunny. She said she was not only Phil's sixth wife but also his widow. She was with him when he died and she'd still be with him if he'd been able to beat the cancer. Her voice faltered and she cleared her throat. In the momentary silence I studied her appearance. Her skin was smooth and clear, her short blond bob perfectly coifed. I wouldn't venture to guess the ages of most of the women in the room, but I'd bet money Sunny was at least ten to twelve years younger than the others.

"I know you all have different memories and experiences of Phil," Sunny said. "But he was my entire world. Every morning when I wake up I thank God we had the time together that we had. I just wish it could've been longer."

At that, the first wife—Peggy—piped up. "Be careful what you wish for, honey. As you can see, Phil wasn't so good when it came to the long haul. The good news is, at least he never got off cheap."

The women around the table nodded.

"Amen," said one.

"You got that right, honey," said another.

Valentine broke in. "Ladies, let's try to keep this to introductions only. We still have a lot of ground to cover."

The next woman spoke with a slight lisp. She said her name was Rita O'Reilly, formerly Rita Wilkerson, and she'd been Phil's second wife. She said that her marriage to Phil had been a short one but they'd managed to stay together long enough to have one child. She finished by saying she had no idea why she, and not her college-age daughter, had been summoned to the reading of Philip's will.

The woman sitting to my right was the blousy blond who'd asked about other heirs before Valentine had had a chance to lay down the ground rules. She introduced herself in a booming voice as Joanie Bush, Phil's third wife. She said she and Phil had been blessed with twins. She said even though they were grown now, she knew the twins missed their father every day.

She said she'd never taken Phil's name when they married because she wanted to keep her professional name. Her cutesy name, stupendous boob job and spikey mass of white-blond hair made me wonder exactly what profession she'd been in.

Finally, it was my turn. I looked around at the assemblage of nuptial train wrecks that had graced my father's bed and said, "My name is Pali Moon. I guess I'm Mr. Wilkerson's daughter. I didn't even know who my father was until just a few minutes ago." I looked across the table at Peggy. "And, I think I'm actually his oldest child. He was only twenty when I was born."

The room began buzzing with side conversations. Joanie Bush, the blond to my right, practically spat at Valentine. "What the hell's going on here? You said Phil specified wives only; no kids."

Valentine put up her palms in an apparent effort to deflect Joanie's anger. "Yes, I know. But that brings us to your earlier question, Miss Bush—"

"It's *Mrs.* Bush," Joanie interrupted. "I remarried, although God knows after Phil it was a miracle I found it in my heart to ever trust a man again."

"Yes, well, *Mrs.* Bush," said Valentine. "As I was saying, we're now ready to address your question regarding the distribution of assets. The information will be provided by means of a video that Mr. Wilkerson made at the time he drafted his will. Of course there's a formal written bequest as well, but he asked me to play the video before making copies of the bequest available."

Valentine went to the corner of the room and fiddled with a DVD player on the TV cart. Then she asked Tim Abbott, the guy standing by the door, if he'd lower the window shades. Tim's upper lip was moist and when he reached up to pull the shade release I saw an underarm sweat patch. Valentine also seemed a little shaky, but I attributed it to calorie-deprivation and working under the scrutiny of a gaggle of greedy women.

When the TV sparked to life I blinked at the brightness in the darkened room. The first image was a vivid blue background with the words "Last Will and Testament of Phillip J. Wilkerson III" on it. Hawaiian slack key guitar music played in the background as the words faded and were replaced by the date 'August 2011' and then the words 'Peace of Paradise, Hawaii' were added.

The blue title slide was replaced by a sweeping view of lawn, cityscape, ocean, and sky. Judging from the city skyline I determined the shot must've been taken from a hill overlooking Honolulu.

The camera panned to reveal a man sitting in a wheelchair on a ground level lanai. Behind him was a wall of glass and to his right a pool of water, probably a fish pond or a reflecting pool.

As the camera zoomed in, I got a good look at my father's face. He had a high forehead with thinning brown hair. His features were pretty average except for a thin, sharp nose. His steely eyes stared back at the camera as if challenging it to judge him. On a small table at his side was a cut-crystal highball glass with a wedge of lime perched on the rim.

He wore what appeared to be an expensive aloha shirt, maybe Tommy Bahama, and light tan slacks. The video seemed to be professionally shot. Smooth panning, good lighting, skillful focusing. I've had to sit through enough poorly-produced wedding videos that I can spot good work when I see it. Wilkerson didn't display even the slightest evidence of uneasiness at being in front of a camera. No anxious twitches or self-conscious smiles. Although he appeared wan and somewhat emaciated, his jowly neckline hinted that at one time he'd probably been overweight.

I shifted in my chair as I took in his face. I'd studied my own facial profile both in photos and in the mirror so I was well-aware my own beak tended more toward hawk than sparrow. And I'd always considered my forehead to be a bit high. I cover it with a fringe of bangs that I cut myself when they extend below my eyebrows. Phil Wilkerson's light brown hair—what was left of it—was the same color as mine if you didn't factor in the peroxide-aided highlights Farrah had talked me into a few weeks back.

The camera went in for a close-up and Phil, aka Coyote Moon, began to speak.

"*Aloha.* My name is Phil Wilkerson. I'm the President and CEO of Island Paradise Cable, the largest provider of cable and Internet services in the Hawaiian Islands. I was born in Portland, Oregon on June seventh, nineteen-fifty-eight. My parents, now deceased, were Gladys and Phillip Wilkerson Junior, of Portland,

Oregon. My father owned Oregon Ferrous and Foundry, a steel mill on the Willamette River. Before moving to Hawaii I enjoyed a comfortable childhood with two loving parents. I had one brother, Robert. He was wounded in the Vietnam War in 1973 and took his own life eight years later." At this Phil bit his lower lip, as if the memory still stung.

I glanced around the dim room. It appeared Phil's family saga was old news to everyone else. But it was certainly new news to me.

He went on. "I attended the University of Oregon in Eugene, the alma mater of Phil Knight, the founder of a little company called Nike. Before college, I took some time off to see the world and I came to Hawaii. I stayed longer than I'd planned. For almost two years, nineteen-seventy-five and seventy-six, I lived a totally carefree life. I spent some time on the north shore of Kaua'i in an area known as Taylor Camp. I've always considered my Taylor Camp days precious. Although I've done well for myself in business, I've never forgotten the many dear friends I made there. "

Many dear friends? My mother was no more to this guy than a *dear friend?* What did that make me—an *acquaintance?* I felt my face flush. The rushing sound in my ears returned and it was so loud and distracting I found it difficult to hear the video. After a few moments of taking in Wilkerson's almost wolfish smile and watching his lips move, I calmed down enough to once again make out what he was saying.

"Since you are viewing this video it means my life has ended. I enjoyed life immensely, but even the sweetest moments must come to a close, and that is why I've called you all together."

At that point he clasped his hands and bowed his head. Then he closed his eyes. We all sat there, waiting. I got the distinct impression this self-indulgent pause in the action was a glimpse into the true character of Phillip James Wilkerson, the Third.

He opened his eyes. At that point, Valentine cleared her throat and got up and went to stand next to Tim Abbott by the door. As I took in Valentine's impassive face and erect posture, I couldn't help but feel she was positioning herself for a quick getaway.

***

Phil Wilkerson stared straight into the camera lens with a thin smile. Then he leaned in and began to speak again.

"To the extent possible, I have done my best to be a good father. I provided a comfortable lifestyle to my children that knew no bounds. Private schools, blow-out birthday parties and lavish Christmas gifts; my children enjoyed it all. Each got a new sports car at sixteen, and a free ride to any college they could get into. And what did I get in return? Drug abuse, disrespect, and calls from the police in the middle of the night. Of my eight children, only one hasn't disappointed me. To my eldest daughter, who now calls herself 'Pali', I want to apologize for my absence in your life. I had my reasons, but now my reasons don't matter. I'm sure whatever justice the good Lord has in store for me will be fair. I felt I had no recourse other than the one I chose."

I squirmed in my chair as he leaned in and nearly touched his nose to the camera lens. "But know this, Pali. Even though I never contacted you I've been watching you. I never lost sight of where you were and what you were doing. I was there when you graduated from the University of Hawaii, and I was pleased when I heard you'd been accepted into the Homeland Security Federal Air Marshal Training program on the mainland. I'm proud of you. You managed to get a college education with no financial or emotional support from either side of your family."

It was getting downright embarrassing as my father blathered on about my life. I felt the gaze of everyone in the room shift from watching the screen to watching me.

"At the time of this video, you'd opened a small business on a neighbor island. Good for you; I hope your business is extremely successful. You're my only child who never asked me for anything. Your brothers and sisters made innumerable demands. It was usually for more than they needed, and in most cases, more than they deserved.

"I'm sure the rest of you watching are wondering when I'll get around to you. In my mind's eye I can imagine you and your offspring toting up the spoils now that the old man's gone. Well, here it is."

There was a collective intake of breath. Phil went on, "During my life I was forced to live with—and even support—bad behavior and lousy decision-making. Certainly, some of the blame falls to me, but not all. Therefore, I'm done with that. With the blessing of my attorney and my accountant I've decided to bequeath my entire estate to two, and only two, beneficiaries. One-half of my total assets will go to my loving wife, Suzanne, or Sunny, as she prefers to be called. The other half will go to my eldest daughter, Pali Moon.

"Throughout my final ordeal Sunny has stood by me without complaint. She asked for little, but gave so much. I love you, Sunny. I owe you everything. Not only for what you've done for me but even more for what you've promised to do for me."

Everyone turned to look at Sunny but she kept her eyes glued to the image on the television.

Phil Wilkerson droned on. "Valentine advised me to make this video so everyone could see that the choice of how I would divide my assets was mine and mine alone. She and Tim Abbott will fill you in on the details. I wish you all a life as wonderful as mine has been. *Aloha* and God bless."

The television screen went dark. Valentine clomped over to the windows and lifted the shades. The sunlit room remained silent for about three seconds. Then all hell broke loose.

8

"These two twits get everything?" shouted Joanie Bush, the aging Anna Nicole Smith-wannabe. She pointed at me with a stiletto-sharp fingernail. "This one didn't even know Phil was her father until an hour ago. And her…" she pointed at Sunny, "just magically appeared in time to rake in a fortune."

"The decedent has the sole vote in deciding who will inherit the estate," said Valentine. "And in this case, at least Mr. Wilkerson made the effort to explain his decision. He appreciated the care his wife Sunny gave him and he was repentant about not being a loving father to Pali."

"Well, excuse me, but he was a lousy father to my two kids," said Peggy Chesterton, wife number one. She turned to me. "Trust me, you didn't miss much. I'm sure my kids would've rather had the money."

While the ex-wives engaged in side conversations, Sunny Wilkerson raised a hand and waited to be called on.

"Yes, Sunny?" said Valentine.

"So, that's it? Pali and I will split the estate?"

"That's it," said Valentine. "Except Mr. Wilkerson requested that you be allowed to live in the Kaua'i property for as long as you wish. The property will not be sold until you want to dispose of it."

"What's the matter, Sunny D?" said Joanie. "Did Phil promise you the whole enchilada? Last I heard Phil was worth thirty million bucks. Are you afraid you won't be able to snag a new boy-toy with a mere fifteen mil?"

Rita, wife number two, smiled at that but the others kept up the glowering.

"This can't be legal," said Peggy. "My kids deserve at least something. I'm gonna call my lawyer."

Joanie shot back, "Oh shut up. My kids are getting screwed as much as yours, but there's not a damn thing we can do about it. One thing about Phil, he always did things legit."

Peggy turned to Sunny. "Well, just the same, don't rack up the credit card bills, sweetie, because I'm not taking this lying down. I want to see what a judge says about Phil cutting my kids off like this."

"Are you deaf?" said Joanie. "A judge can't do anything. It's up to these two to make this right." She pointed at me and then Sunny.

I grabbed my beach bag purse and pushed back my chair. Joanie reached over and gripped my upper arm. Her near-lethal fingernails bit into my flesh but I refused to give her the satisfaction of an *ouch*.

"Listen up, missy," she said. "You can prance on out of here thumbing your nose at your brothers and sisters or you can do the right thing. What'll it be?"

I stared her down. Even if I'd been giving serious thought to being generous, there was no way I'd allow her to think she'd bullied me into it.

"Let me go," I said in my best CLC voice. "I'll give you two seconds to think about it."

"Oh, and then what? You sound like your idiot father. All threats and bluster, but in the end he always paid up." She released my arm. "You know this is wrong."

Peggy piped up. "Oh give it up, Joanie. She didn't know Phil, but she's a chip off the old block. The only way our kids are going to get anything is to fight this in court."

Peggy got up and left. Before she could pull the door closed behind her, Joanie grabbed her stuff and followed her out. Rita and Linda left soon after. Tim Abbott mumbled to Valentine that he'd see everyone out.

"Is it true my father was worth thirty million dollars?" I said to Valentine.

"That's an estimate," she said. "What with probate costs, real estate commissions and taxes, Tim tells me the approximate net value will be more like twenty to twenty-five million."

"That means around ten million each?" said Sunny.

"At least, maybe more." Valentine looked pensive. "Although if Peggy actually does contest the will, we may be looking at higher attorney fees than we anticipated."

"I can understand why she's angry about me getting anything," I said. "After all, I just showed up out of nowhere. But what's her problem with Sunny? Isn't Hawaii a community property state?"

"It is," said Valentine. "And Phil was clear he wanted Sunny's half to be treated as community property, for tax reasons. But don't worry. The will is iron-clad. Once the initial shock wears off I doubt if we'll hear anything further from those ladies."

"I'm not so sure," said Sunny. "Peggy's family name carries a lot of weight around here."

"You two have a lot to talk about," Valentine said, getting up to leave. "Feel free to stay as long as you like. I'll be in touch regarding probate court. It'd be best if you could both plan to be there." She went out and closed the door.

Sunny and I stared at each other across the table.

"How long were you married?" I said.

Sunny blew out a breath. "Oh great. Now you're joining the lynch mob?"

"No, sorry. That didn't come out right. It's just that you look quite a bit younger than my father."

"I am. But to be fair, by the time your father made that video he was already pretty sick. He looked older than he was. He was only fifty-four when he died."

She fiddled with a plain pearl earring in her earlobe. "And as far as my age, I turned thirty last winter. I guess that makes me a few years younger than you."

I nodded.

"Do you have a problem with that?"

"Look," I said. "I came here this morning expecting to hear something about my mom. She died when I was five and I was never told much about how she died. Now I find out I had a missing father who's been gouging me for cable TV service for the past fifteen years and who died and left me a pile of cash. It's all kind of surreal, you know?"

"Tell you what," said Sunny. "Let's go someplace to talk. You like shave ice?"

***

As I went down the two flights of wooden stairs I felt my hand gripping the handrail and my feet on the treads but that's about all. What had just happened? And why had I agreed to get shave ice and hang out with my father's trophy-wife widow? More than anything I just wanted to locate my rental car and get back to Poipu as fast as possible.

I didn't want ten million dollars. And I certainly didn't want seven pissed-off half-siblings. And most of all, it creeped me out to learn my father had been lurking in the shadows all along and he'd never once shown his face or owned up to his responsibilities.

"You know," I said when we made it to the ground floor. "Can I take a rain check on the shave ice? I'm feeling a little overwhelmed right now and I need some alone time."

"Sure, we can talk later. Where are you staying?"

"I'm down in Poipu with my boyfriend but we're flying back to Maui this afternoon. We both need to get back to work tomorrow."

She smiled. "Actually, if you think about it, only one of you *needs* to get back to work."

"Not if Peggy has her way."

"No worries. Valentine's right, the will is solid. The truth is, Peggy never got over Phil. She and her father were always lurking in the background. Phil put up with it because he needed the mayor's support for his business. But your father wanted the two of us to have the money and we're getting it. End of story."

I nodded. "I guess I just need to go home. I'm kind of in shock."

"Yeah, I get it. How about this? When Valentine sets up the date for probate court, I'd like you to stay up at the house with me. I've got a great little *ohana* guest house, so you'll have privacy. You could even bring your boyfriend if you want."

I bit my lip.

"It's okay; you don't have to decide right now," Sunny went on. "Just keep it in mind. Here's my card. Call me if you want to talk."

She handed me a pale lavender card that said, 'Healing Waters Spa' along with her name and the words Masseuse and Aesthetician.

"You're a masseuse?" I said.

"I was. That's how I met your dad. I'm also an aesthetician. I didn't work on any of them myself, but three of those so-called 'ladies' you just met upstairs are clients at the spa."

"Did you know I even existed before meeting me today?" I asked.

"Of course. Dying men don't keep secrets."

9

I got in the rental car but didn't start the engine. Instead, I sat and stared at my cell phone. I tried to call Hatch, but my hands were shaking so much it took a few tries before the call went through.

"Hey babe," he said. "How'd it go? You okay?"

"I'm fine," I said. "No problem. Everything's good." I'm a lousy liar and Hatch picked up on it right away.

"You don't sound fine. You sound freaked. What happened?"

"I can't really talk about it now," I said. I watched as people went in and came out of the Ching Young shopping center. The archway leading into the center brought up a vague memory of coming there with my mother.

"Are you okay to drive?"

"I'm fine. But before I come back to Poipu I'd like to drive up to Ke'e Beach for a quick look around. That's where they held my mom's memorial service. I want to pay my respects."

"You sure you want to do that alone?"

"Yeah. I'm good. By the way, how was your baseball game?"

"We smoked 'em. Nine to two."

"Good. Where are you now? I can hardly hear you."

"We're at the pizza place. Say, are you sure you're okay to drive?"

"I told you; I'm fine. I'll be back in plenty of time to make our flight."

"Okay, but give me a call me if you need me to come get you. I'm sure I could snag a ride from one of these guys. Trust me, they'd rather take me up there to get you now than have to shovel your mangled carcass into a body bag later."

That's what I love about Hatch. He always knows how to make me feel better.

***

The road out to Ke'e Beach was curvy and narrow, but there wasn't much traffic. It was just after one o'clock on a Wednesday afternoon. Too late for surfers and way too early for sunset-watchers. I went over a series of one-lane bridges and past gaping dry caves. But when I got to the end of the road at Ke'e Beach I was surprised to find the parking lot completely full. And, for a quarter mile, cars were parked head-to-toe alongside the road.

I pulled into a spot reserved for emergency vehicles and headed down to the beach. I wouldn't be long. I'd heard a lot about Taylor Camp by eavesdropping on my Auntie Mana as she told stories at family gatherings. I'd looked it up on the Internet and learned the camp had been located between Limahuli Stream and what was now Ke'e Beach Park. It mentioned a trail on the *mauka* or inland edge of the park that led to where the camp had once been. Sure enough, I found a wide trail to the right of the park restrooms. After about a hundred yards, I had the strange sensation I was being followed. I turned in a complete circle but couldn't see anyone. I continued down the trail. The vegetation became thick, with towering trees and low scrub blocking out the sunlight. Philodendron vines snaked up the trunks making it hard to tell where one tree stopped and another started. I came to a copse of mature trees at least fifty to sixty feet tall. Were these trees where the hippies had built their tree houses? It seemed impossible to imagine. I stood in the center of the thicket and closed my eyes and tried to still my mind. But as I breathed in the scent of ocean and rotting leaves, I once again got the sensation of someone watching. I snapped my eyes open and looked around. There were a few people far down on the beach, but no one looked my way.

I'd been barely a toddler when Taylor Camp was shut down. The tree in front of me had three huge branches that formed a crook. It would have made a great foundation for a tree house. The main platform could've spanned the branches and extended to nearby trees.

The hippies at Taylor Camp were tolerated by the locals, but just barely. After more than a few run-ins with the law regarding their rampant drug use, the authorities decided it was time to shut the place down. They evicted the squatters and came in and burned the camp.

When we moved from Taylor Camp my mom had a new man in her life, my brother's father. I'd called him Uncle Ricky or Robby—something like that. But right around the time my mother died, Uncle What's-His-

Name disappeared, just like my dad. I don't recall ever mourning his departure. I guess it was because with my mother gone my life was pretty much already in free-fall.

I walked out of the trees and out to the beach. I looked to the horizon, where I'd last seen the surfboards and canoes taking my mom's ashes out to sea.

"Love you, Mom. I'm sorry I didn't go on that last journey with you. But I've never forgotten." I put my hand over my heart like I was saying the Pledge of Allegiance. Then I felt the presence watching me again and, embarrassed, I put my hand back down.

I whispered, "Godspeed to you, Mom, wherever you are." Then I jogged back to where I'd parked the car.

***

The drive to Poipu turned out to be easier than I'd imagined. Maybe it's because there's only one way to get from Hanalei to the South Shore of Kaua'i and it's an easy, mostly-two lane road that follows the coastline. There were few distractions and little traffic. I hadn't eaten lunch but I wasn't hungry.

"Hey babe," said Hatch as I came into the lobby. He got up from a comfy-looking chair and hugged me.

I looked up at him. Staring into his anxious brown eyes I felt my throat start to close up. My eyes burned.

"Let's go to the room," I croaked. I made it through the lobby and down the walkway before I felt a tickle on my cheek. I swiped away a tear. Then my nose started in. When I snuffed it up, Hatch dug around in his pocket and handed me a wadded-up tissue.

"It's kinda mashed up, but it's clean," he said.

"*Mahalo*," I said. "I must be getting a cold or something."

We got to the room and as Hatch closed the door behind us, something inside me shattered. Hatch led me to the sofa and we sat down. He put an arm around my shoulders. I leaned into him, hoping to blot out the memory of the last four hours.

After a few minutes of silence, I launched into an account of why Valentine Fabares had asked me to come to Kaua'i

"The lawyer read your dad's will?" Hatch said. "And you say he left you some money?"

I'd soft-peddled the enormity of my inheritance. I still hadn't decided how I felt about it, and I didn't know how long probate might take, so the less said the better.

"Yeah. He was a businessman. Owned a company here in the islands."

"What was his name?"

"Phillip J. Wilkerson, the Third."

"*The Third*? Boy howdy, sounds like you come from some upper-crust folks."

"Either that or my grandparents were too lazy to come up with an original name."

"Maybe that's why your father got so creative when he named you."

I blew out a sigh.

"You say he lived here in Hawaii?"

"I guess so. He said he started his company in the eighties."

"Then why didn't he come get you after your mom died?"

Good question, but not one I cared to ponder. "From the looks of things, ditching people was something he was really good at," I said.

"Oh?" Hatch leaned away and raised an eyebrow.

"The guy had *six* wives. Five exes and a widow. The widow is a thirty-year-old masseuse who took care of him while he was dying. There were so many women at the meeting I had to take notes to keep them all straight." I grabbed my purse and pulled out the notebook. "Wife number five didn't bother to show up. Numbers two and four seemed okay, but number one was completely full of herself and number three looked like a hooker."

"Wow. And your dad never married your mom, right?"

"What are you getting at, Hatch?" When I was a kid, I'd always feared being called 'the b-word.' Now that I was a grown woman 'the b-word' stood for something entirely different. At least with the second 'b-word' I had some control over whether it was justified or not.

"Don't get your back up," he said. "What I mean is if they'd been married he would've had *seven* wives. Kind of a record. But maybe that's why he included you in his will. He didn't do right by your mom, so he wanted to do right by you."

"Maybe."

"Did you find out if you have any newfound brothers or sisters?"

"Oh yeah. He had seven other kids besides me."

"Seven? Wow, that's great."

"You think?"

"Sure. You've finally got a big *ohana*. Isn't that what you always wanted?"

"I guess." I didn't want to go into how Phil had set it up so there was zero chance I'd ever be invited to family gatherings or get to play auntie to any nieces or nephews. My pariah status would come out soon enough. "The last wife, Sunny, was really friendly. She invited me to stay with her when I come back for probate court."

"That's good. Hey, did you have any lunch?" he said. "I meant to bring you some pizza but those guys were animals. Ate every last slice. Let's go grab something down by the pool."

At the poolside grill I ordered a cheeseburger with curly fries. I don't usually allow myself to eat stuff like that, but the morning's events had kicked my self-discipline to the curb.

While we ate, a guy in his late twenties came to the pool holding hands with a tiny girl in a pink polka-dotted swimsuit. They got in the water and the little girl clung to the guy's back while he hauled her around.

"More, daddy, more," squealed the little girl.

"In a little bit," said the dad. "But first I'm going to teach you to swim. First, you need to put your face in the water."

The little girl looked up at him and shook her head. Her wet curls threw off water droplets like a dog shaking itself after a bath.

"Don't be afraid, honey. I'm right here," he said.

After a couple of chin-deep efforts praised by her father, she finally dunked her entire head under.

"Good girl," he crowed, grabbing her when she popped back up. "I'm so proud of you, Ava."

I pushed my plate away. "You know, I'm probably the only kid in Hawaii who never learned to swim."

Hatch shot me a pained look. "Oh come on. It's not like you to play the victim card."

"I know," I said. "I'm just saying."

"Message received. Your dad was a jerk. Well, remind me someday to tell you about my old man. If misery loves company, you'll love my company when we compare your AWOL dad to my drunk and disorderly one."

"Point taken."

"Hey, look at the time," said Hatch. "We've got a plane to catch."

We packed up and headed to the airport. The flight to Maui was uneventful except for me garnering *stink eye* from the flight attendant when my phone went off during the 'in the event of an emergency' announcement.

I checked the caller ID before flicking off the phone

"Who was it?" said Hatch.

"Just Farrah. She's probably just checking to make sure we made our flight. I suppose when you live your entire life in one building, keeping track of everyone else's comings and goings is a big deal. I'll call her when we land."

We retrieved Hatch's car from long-term parking. He gallantly opened the passenger door for me before going around to the driver's side. "You want to go straight home or stop off at your shop?"

"Would you mind dropping me at Farrah's? I need to tell her about the trip. Since you're on shift in the morning you probably shouldn't wait. I'll ask Steve to come down and get me later."

"I really don't mind waiting."

"That's sweet, but I've been gone three days. Farrah will demand a minute by minute accounting."

We pulled in front of the Gadda da Vida Grocery and I leaned over and gave Hatch a kiss. I went for the real thing, not a little 'thanks for everything' peck on the mouth.

"Whoa. Maybe I should wait for you after all," he said.

"No, that's got to keep you going until this weekend. I've got a ton of stuff to catch up on at work. I've got that big Lindberg wedding on the Fourth and I'm way behind in doing my vendor follow-up calls. If Eleanor catches even a whiff of me slacking off she'll probably demand I cut my commission in half."

"Okay, but we're still on for Saturday, right? I've got that firefighter awards dinner in Wailea."

"You never told me, are you up for an award?"

"Who knows? But it's at the ballroom of the Grand Wailea. Award or no award it'll be first class all the way."

"It's a date."

I went inside. I was surprised to see Beatrice working the counter so late in the evening. Beatrice is an ancient lady who often comes in while Farrah takes lunch. She occasionally helps out if Farrah has a tarot reading in the afternoon, but I've never seen her at the store after dark.

"Hey Bea, how's it shakin'?" I said. I talked loud, since Bea has a hearing problem. She says it's only in one ear, but from what I can tell neither ear works any better than the other one.

"A snake? You seen a snake?" Bea looked horrified. "We gotta kill it. No good to have snakes in the islands."

"No," I said waving my hand. I went up to her and talked as if I was in an elocution contest. "No snake. I just came in to say 'hi'. Do you know where Farrah is?"

Bea scrutinized my face. "She say she not feeling so good. I'm working all day. I gotta sit down sometimes on this little stool. You know, I got the arthur in my knees."

I nodded and pointed at the ceiling rather than ask if Farrah was upstairs in her apartment.

Bea nodded.

"*Mahalo*," I said. "I'll go on up."

"Oh, good luck to you too, Pali."

I went out the back door and climbed the stairs to Farrah's apartment. A searing blue-white security light came on when I hit the fourth stair. I knocked and waited for her to scrutinize me through the peep hole.

As soon as the door opened I knew something was up.

10

The unmistakable odor of 'baby'—wet diapers, baby powder and milk—was all over Farrah. She looked like she'd been working in the cane fields all day. Matted hair, haggard face, slumped shoulders.

"What's going on?" I said.

"Come in. This is going to totally blow your mind."

In daytime, Farrah's apartment is always dimly lit because she's covered her windows in fake stained glass contact paper. When the sun goes down she usually turns on a few lights but there were no lights on when I went inside. But even in the near-darkness it didn't take long for me to locate the source of the smell. A tiny baby, most probably a newborn, was lying on a tattered blanket in the middle of the room. It wore nothing but a disposable diaper and a benign smile. The kid was half-heartedly kicking its arms and legs. I'm not exactly a 'baby person.' To me, the little creature looked like a bug on its back trying to right itself.

"What's going on?" I said again. "Can you turn on a light here?"

She snapped on a table lamp. "You leave for a few days and see what happens?" she said. She was positively beaming.

Okay, this was a first, even for Farrah. Last year she'd mistaken the gender of her dog, Sir Lipton, and 'he'd' had puppies. I'd found that almost unbelievable, but Farrah not realizing she was pregnant and about to give birth? Not even Farrah's ubiquitous billowy *mu'u mu'u* dresses could have concealed *that* state of affairs.

"Farrah? What the *hell* is going on?"

"Okay, he's not mine," she said. "Well, he's mine, but not technically. Yet."

"Have you still got some of that 'Awake' tea?" I said. "I'm gonna make us some. And then you're going to tell me everything." I went to Farrah's miniscule kitchenette and filled the tea kettle. Then I rummaged through her bread box-sized cupboard and found a tea tin with a picture of a guy with sunbeams shooting out of his head. The label read, 'AWAKE TEA, Not Your Grandma's Cuppa'.

By the time the tea had steeped, the baby had nodded off. I carried two cups into the living room dodging cast-off clothes, a heap of wadded-up bath towels, and Lipton's slobbery dog toys.

"This isn't the most sanitary environment for a baby," I whispered. "Does the mother know you live like this?"

"I'm the mother around here," said Farrah in a hissed voice. "I'm exposing Baby to the rigors of this Earthly world. How can he build a strong immune system if his body doesn't learn to make peace with normal physical surroundings?"

"This goes way beyond 'normal'," I said looking down at the matted carpet that had never known the whirr of a vacuum cleaner and the dog hair-encrusted blanket that had never felt the wet of a washing machine. "This is like a giant petri dish. Remember that scary stuff we grew in high school biology?"

"I don't dig your harsh remarks but I'm going to ignore them because I need your *kokua*—your help," Farrah said.

"Before I'll offer to help, I need some answers. Where's this baby's mother?"

"I don't know. Yesterday morning when I went down to work, there he was. Like baby Moses in the rushes."

I was surprised by Farrah's biblical reference. As far as I knew, she wasn't one to attend church, let alone read the Bible. But she was an ordained minister of an online spiritual community, "The Church of Spirit and Light." She'd become a minister so she could conduct wedding ceremonies for "Let's Get Maui'd", but no doubt she'd had to learn at least some measure of mainstream Christian/Judaic beliefs to pass the final exam.

"This baby was abandoned?"

"Bummer, right? Here's the note." She handed me a note written in childish block letters on three-hole notebook paper.

Grocery store lady—Please take my boy. You can give him a new name if you want. Since you have lots of food I now he wont go hungary. Tell him his mama loves him very much.

The mother had misspelled a few words, but the message was clear.

"Wow, Farrah, you need to report this to the police," I said.

"You, of all people, want to see this little guy dumped in the system?" Farrah picked up the baby and clutched his damp diaper-clad body to her breast. With clutching hands the baby rooted around the bosom of her *mu'u mu'u* trying to figure out how to get to what lay beneath.

"Look, Farrah, you can't just keep a baby because some pathetic woman left it on your doorstep. There are laws."

"This is Hawaii. You weren't handed over to 'the man' when your mom passed. Your Auntie Mana took you in. No social workers, no judges, no nuthin' like that. So don't go all establishment on me here, Pali Moon. Help me figure out how I can keep my baby."

***

By the time we'd finished the Awake tea, we'd come up with a short term plan. I offered mother and baby safe haven at my house in Hali'imaile for a few days to get away from the prying eyes and ears of the customers at Farrah's store. Beatrice wouldn't be a problem because she's practically deaf, but it wouldn't be long before a customer would claim they were sure they heard a baby crying upstairs and want to investigate.

"I've got to clear this with Steve first," I said. "He's coming down to pick me up in a few minutes. But don't worry, it's just a formality."

Steve arrived twenty minutes later. On the drive to Hali'imaile I told him about Farrah's baby.

"Are you kidding?" he said. "How am I supposed to put up with poopy diaper smell? And waking up to bawling at three o'clock in the morning? It's just not in my nature to tolerate stuff like that."

"Look, Steve, I've heard what sounds like 'bawling' coming from your room at three o'clock in the morning and I've never said a word."

He whipped his head around and looked at me aghast.

"Okay, I'm just kidding," I said. "But seriously, Farrah has to have somewhere to go while she figures this out. If a customer hears the baby and calls the police, not only will she get in trouble for having the baby, but she'll get kicked out of her apartment. It was condemned, remember? No one knows she lives up there."

"Oh bull," said Steve. "The whole town knows she's up there, including the cops. They don't hassle her because they need her to run the Gadda. If she left, then the weed-heads would try to bum rides off tourists to get down to Kahului for their Cheetos or their rolling papers. The last thing the cops want to deal with is some stinky dope-smokers hassling Dot and Bob from Minneapolis."

We compromised with me offering to give up my downstairs bedroom to Farrah. I'd move into the guest room adjacent to Steve's bedroom on the second floor. "With the two of them downstairs you won't hear a thing. And I've laid down the law with Farrah about housekeeping. Diapers will be disposed of properly and bottles and nipples will be washed and put away promptly."

"*Nipples?*" said Steve. He shimmied in disgust. "Let's avoid mentioning stuff like that, okay? I won't be able to get that image out of my head for a week."

"Oh get over it. You were a baby once."

"Not hardly. I sprang full-bearded from an Abercrombie & Fitch catalog."

"You're not 'full-bearded' now," I said, reaching over to stroke Steve's pathetic Brad Pitt goatee. He'd spent a small fortune on online products including a 'facial hair stimulator' that looked suspiciously like a vibrator I'd come across at a rather tawdry bridal fair.

I went on. "Please act nice. Farrah's been through a lot this past year."

Steve reluctantly agreed. "How long is the rug rat going to live with us?"

"Hard to say. I'm going to get in touch with Sifu Doug's lawyer brother, James. I have to play it cool, since Farrah doesn't want 'the man' involved. But I'm worried the baby's mother will pop back into the picture after she comes down from whatever she was hopped up on when she ditched the kid. If that happens, Farrah will be heartbroken."

"Farrah's not planning on keeping the kid forever, is she?" Steve's voice zoomed up a couple of octaves.

"Seems that's what she's thinking. But it's not like she came across a kitten in her dryer vent. She's going to have to jump through some hoops to be able to keep him."

"Whoa. But you just said they weren't going to stay for very long. I mean, we all love Farrah. No argument there. But a droopy drawers kid pitching food off a high chair and the TV blasting Barney the Dinosaur when I'm trying to sleep in? Ugh."

"Don't worry. The kid will be long gone before he ever needs a high chair."

"Pinkie swear?" said Steve.

I held up my pinkie finger. "Swear."

"On another subject, tell me what you found out about your mom over in Kaua'i."

"Nothing."

"Nothing?" he said. "Then why did the lawyer make you go over there?"

"To let me know my SOB father had died."

"Wow, you found your father? Who was he?"

"I just told you. He was an SOB and now he's dead. End of story."

11

On Thursday morning I got up before dawn and went down to the Palace of Pain, the martial arts studio where I work out. Because I'd had so many weddings in June I'd been spotty in getting in my workouts. I hoped it was early enough that my instructor, Sifu Doug, wouldn't be in yet.

No such luck. His car was parked in the alley.

"Hey, stranger," he said when I came inside.

"Hey, Sifu. I've been over in Kaua'i." I left it vague, hoping he'd think I'd been off-island for most of June.

"How long were you over there?"

"I just got back yesterday."

"Okay, don't tell me. But you know if you don't keep up your practice you'll get soft." He nodded toward the wall where my picture hung alongside the five other black belts, all of them guys, who trained at PoP, "You know lots of *keiki* girls look up to you."

"Sorry, Sifu. But this was a busy month."

"Then I better let you get to it. You gonna go through your forms?" It wasn't a question, it was an order.

"Yes, Sifu."

"All of them?"

"Yes, sir."

I'd planned to stay about an hour but it turned out to be closer to two. I took a quick shower and started to head out when I noticed Sifu Doug sitting in his office. No time like the present. I poked my head inside.

"You got a minute?" I said.

"Sure, just move that stuff off the chair."

I sat down on a metal folding chair across from Doug. Three years ago when I first laid eyes on him he'd scared the daylights out of me. Former Army Ranger, chiseled good looks, eyes that bore into opponents with such ferocity that he'd won more than a few fights by sheer intimidation.

"What's happenin'?" he said.

"I've got a problem."

He smiled. "Pali, you know I love you like a *sista*, but just once I'd like you to come into my office carrying something other than a problem."

"I know; I apologize. How about I make you some cookies or something?"

"I got a wife for that," he said. "But next time you hear some gossip, or a good joke, you come tell me. I get first dibs."

I thought about my meeting yesterday. Talk about a joke. My father had been Hawaii's cable mogul and I found out I had six siblings. And from the looks of things I'd be coming into some serious cash real soon. But I wasn't there to talk about me.

"You got it, Sifu. Next time I get something juicy you'll be the first to know."

"Okay, so what's on your mind?"

"All of this is just conjecture, okay? A total what-if."

"Got it."

"If someone asks someone else to raise their kid for them, is it legal?"

"You know it is. We got *hanai* kids all over these islands. You were a *hanai* kid yourself, weren't you?"

"Right. But my mother was dead and my father was gone. There was nobody to tell my Auntie Mana she couldn't take me in."

"What are you getting at? You got that biological clock tickin' and you thinkin' of snatchin' a kid? That is totally *not* legal, believe me." He smiled but his eyes held a squint of concern.

"No, no, nothing like that. Like I said, this is just a 'what if'. But if a mother came to me and asked me to raise her kid because she couldn't, could I do it?"

"I think so. That's how *hanai* works. You both agree. On the mainland I think they call it an open adoption. But you'd have to ask my brother James about the stuff you gotta do to make it all legal. He's the lawyer."

"What happens if you don't do it all legal?"

"Pali, I don't know what you're getting at here. But if you don't do it legal, then I suppose if the parents change their mind they could come after you. It could be bad. They could demand you give the kid back. They could call you a kidnapper. You'd have to ask James, but kidnapping's a serious crime. Maybe even federal."

"Yeah, I think that's right."

"You want me to ask James to give you a call?" he said. "Or is this all still 'what if'?"

"I'd appreciate a call. I'm working at lot, so please have him call me at the shop, not at home."

"Will do." He got up and extended a hand. We did his little 'man shake' thing with a few fist bumps and slides and then he slapped me on the shoulder. "Take care of yourself, Pali. No good comes from messing around with the law." He winked. "You think you want a kid? I bet I could talk Lani into handing over one of ours."

***

I went to my shop and started sorting through the mound of mail that had come through the slot while I was gone. Most of it was junk mail and catalogs, but there were also some vendor bills from all the weddings I'd done that month.

I felt restless and hungry so I went next door for a yogurt.

"Hey, Bea," I yelled as I went in. "Still working, I see."

"Uh-huh. I don' know what's wrong with Farrah. Last night somebody tell me they hear cryin' upstairs. She okay when you went up there?"

"Yeah, it was probably just Sir Lipton whining."

"Winning? Did that dog win somethin'? That's a smart dog, I guess. But all I ever see is it do its business in the alley and then go back up the stairs. They give prizes for that?"

I got up close and talked slowly. "I think it was Farrah's dog making the noise."

"Oh yeah. Prob'ly wanted to be let out."

I bought my yogurt and went to my shop and called Steve. "I don't know what to do. I've got a million things to do to catch up, but I've got to get Farrah out of her apartment. It can't wait until the weekend. Somebody at the store heard the baby crying last night."

He sighed so loud I had to hold the phone away from my ear.

"Let me get back to you," he said.

Right after I hung up, the phone rang again. "That was quick," I said.

"What was quick, dear?" It was Eleanor.

"Oh, sorry, Eleanor. I thought you were someone else."

"Who else would I be, dear?"

This wasn't starting out well.

"It's great to hear from you, Eleanor. I'm working on your wedding even as we speak."

"You and Charles need to talk," she said.

That'd be a first. Up to that point, Charles had been more like a ventriloquist dummy than a participant in his own wedding.

"Sure. When would he like to meet?"

"He doesn't know about it yet. You need to call him."

"Okay…" I hoped she'd fill in more blanks, but she stayed uncharacteristically silent. "Eleanor, do you have a number where I can reach him?"

"Just call his room. I think he's there now. Room one-three-one. Same place as me."

She hung up.

I looked up the hotel name on Charles and Eleanor's consultation folder. They were staying at an upscale resort in Wailea. I called and asked to speak to Mr. Charles Lindberg in room one-thirty-one. I figured I'd better say the room number so they wouldn't think it was a crank call involving the other Charles Lindbergh.

"Lindberg," Charles barked when he picked up the phone. I realized I'd never heard his voice before. It sounded more commanding than his chubby bald presence let on.

"Hello Mr. Lindberg," I said. "This is Pali Moon, your wedding planner. I'm calling because—"

He cut me off. "You're calling because the bitch made you call."

"Uh, I…" What could I say?

"Look," he said. "You seem like a nice enough kid. This has nothing to do with you. Tell her I won't go along with it. That's the message. *I'm not going to do it, bitch.*" He hung up.

I slowly put the receiver in the phone set. Their wedding was in six days. Not good. Not good at all.

12

Ten minutes later my shop phone rang again. I answered, hoping it was Charles Lindberg regretfully recanting his message. It wasn't. It was Steve.

"I've got some people lined up," he said.

"Have you offered them blindfolds and cigarettes?"

"Very funny. No, I've got some guys who've offered to help move Farrah."

"When?"

"Right now. I'm coming down there to pick you both up. Tell Farrah to be ready in twenty."

By the time he arrived at the shop he'd softened a little. "You know, ever since that sitcom 'Modern Family' showed those two guys adopting a baby it's been *tres tres chic* for gay men to do the family thing," he said. "But I'm not falling for it. It's a fad. But if Farrah wants a kid, okay I'll go along. I've snagged a crib, a bunch of baby crap like bouncy things and stuffed, uh, stuff. Steven's sister even sent over some baby clothes."

I hugged him. "Big, big *mahalo*, Steve. Farrah will be thrilled."

"I'm sure she will. Anyway, a guy I know from the B & C who's got a pick-up offered to haul the big stuff. He's already on his way so we need to get moving."

"You're the best," I said.

We started toward the stairs to Farrah's apartment. "But we have a deal, right?" he said. "No high chair."

"Both mother and child will be long gone before a high chair is necessary."

When we got to the house Steve's friend, Levi, was already there. I'd never met Levi before, but he was a looker. I'm sure he'd broken a few women's hearts who didn't have the effective 'gaydar' I'd acquired since Steve had come into my life.

"Nice to meet you, ma'am," said Levi as we shook hands. He was one of those cowboy types that some gay men and a lot of women really go for. 'Cowboy' isn't my thing. I lean toward guys with a more conventional style, but I could certainly see how those strip-tease eyes and unruly shock of blond hair could get the juices flowing.

Levi and Steve hauled in the parts to the baby crib. Farrah said not to worry about putting it together because she wanted to do it later. Then she ripped open a box I'd brought in and she started oohing and awing over the tiny clothes.

"Isn't this fab?" she said, holding up a pale yellow 'onesie' with an embroidered monkey on the front.

"What would be 'fab' is you offering to help me lug in these boxes. There are three or four more out there."

"I can't leave Baby," she said. Baby was fast asleep on a blanket on the floor. Thanks to Steve, at least it was a clean blanket.

Sir Lipton stood by the front door, panting. She'd worn herself out running back and forth from truck to house accompanying each load of goods.

"What's the kid's name?" said Levi pointing to the sleeping baby.

"I think it's 'Baby'," I said.

"The poor kid doesn't have a name?" Levi looked puzzled. "Why not?"

Uh-oh. Steve and I exchanged a glance. Leave it to a cowboy to point out the eight-hundred pounds of BS in the middle of our living room.

"He's got a name," Farrah said in a huffy tone. "It's simply not common knowledge yet."

"Huh?" said Levi.

"I've named him, but I'm waiting for the stars to properly align before I speak it to the Universe. There's a time for every purpose under heaven, you know."

"When will the stars align?" I said. I didn't want to seem pushy, but I was hoping she'd say, 'when I've been granted legal guardianship' or something along those lines. Instead, she said, "When Aries is in ascendance and Libra in retrograde."

Seemed the guardianship thing was too much to hope for.

With Farrah and Baby settled in, Levi roared away in his truck. Steve had given him a six-pack of Bikini Blonde Lager from the Maui Brewing Company for his trouble.

"He used a quarter tank of gas and two hours of his time you give him a measly six-pack?" I said.

"No worries. Levi's easy. He's new in town and doesn't know the ropes. I promised I'd introduce him around."

"What is this, the rainbow coalition mafia? You gotta have 'introductions' and learn 'the ropes'?"

"Hey, not everyone qualifies to hang out with us. I keep it strictly friends-only. That way, if anybody messes up, the injured party knows I'll do something about it."

"Sure, Guido, whatever," I said.

I offered to buy him lunch since he'd offered to drive me down to my shop in Pa'ia to pick up my car.

"I really appreciate you going along with this baby thing," I said as we hunkered into a big basket of fish and chips at the Pa'ia Fish Market.

"Remember, this isn't long-term. They're both history before the kid needs a high chair," he said. "You pinkie swore."

"I'm worried Farrah's time with this baby will be way short of a high chair," I said. "I talked to Sifu Doug and he freaked me out talking about kidnapping. He offered to call his brother. Hopefully James can give Farrah some legal advice on what she needs to do."

"Couldn't Farrah just go the *hanai* route? I mean, your Auntie Mana raised you and your brother as *hanai* kids without being legally adopted."

"True. But it wasn't like Auntie Mana just glommed on to us. First off, we were older and we knew her. And I'm sure my mom's friends all spoke up for Mana with the authorities. Farrah doesn't even know who the mother is. It's totally different."

"Would you go to bat for Farrah?"

"Of course. That's why I asked Sifu Doug to call the lawyer. But James is an officer of the court. He can't play

'Let's Make a Deal' with a human being. He's got to follow the rules."

"What do you think will happen?"

I shrugged. "I know what I'd like to have happen. But we're talking about Farrah. She tends to turn left when the sign points right. I'm just hoping she'll come around and do what she needs to do. Otherwise, I'm afraid this whole thing could turn out to be pretty painful."

"For everybody," he said.

"Yeah, for everybody."

We finished our fish and chips in silence. I thanked him again for helping Farrah move in and then I went to my shop. When I got inside, the phone message light was blinking. I punched in the code for my voicemail and learned I had a message from an hour earlier.

It was Eleanor. "Pali," she wailed. "Where are you? How could you abandon me in my hour of need? Get back to me right away."

I called the hotel and asked for her room.

When Eleanor answered, her voice was so cold I thought the phone might ice over "Do you think you could find time in your *busy* day to see me?" she said.

"Certainly. Do you want me to come down there or do you want to meet here at the shop?"

"I think since I'm the *paying* customer you should make the effort to come to me," she said.

"No worries. I'm on my way. Would you like us to meet in the lobby or in your room?"

"What's with all the questions?" she said. "This is an emergency. Get your ass down here!"

I locked up and got into my forlorn little green Geo Metro. I'd promised myself over and over that as soon as I could swing it I'd buy a new ride. A flicker of recollection of yesterday's meeting shot through me and I realized I might be able to go car shopping in the very near future. That put a smile on my face even though I was on my way to handle my least favorite part of my job: run interference between a cranky bride and her reluctant groom.

I pulled up near the Grand King Kamehameha Resort and Spa and parked on the street. No way would I subject myself to the stares and eye rolls of valet parking. And besides, I had a hunch after my meeting with Eleanor the last thing I'd want is to be hanging around waiting for a valet to bring my car around.

"*Aloha* and welcome to the Grand King Kamehameha," said the doorman as he pulled the heavy glass and brass door open for me. "May I direct you to your destination?"

I wanted to tell him my destination was a rude dressing down by an overwrought senior citizen and ask him where he'd suggest that take place, but instead I smiled and said I knew the way.

I called Eleanor's room from the house phone.

"It took you long enough," she said. "Come on up."

I took the elevator to the fourth floor. As I walked down to her room, I realized her room number was at the very end of the hall. A suite. A really big, really spendy suite.

She pulled the door open so quickly I was sure she'd been peering out the peephole as I came down the hallway. Good thing I hadn't been picking my nose—not that I'd ever pick my nose in public, but even so.

"Now what do you suggest we do?" said Eleanor as she turned and went into the enormous living area of the suite. She plopped down in an overstuffed armchair while I took in the view. It was even more beautiful than the view Hatch and I had had in Poipu. Eleanor's suite was smack dab on the ocean with the island of Lana'i clearly outlined on the horizon. The sky was deep blue with only a single puffy cloud to give it dimension. How in the world could someone be having a hissy fit with that kind of God-given beauty laid out in front of them?

"Catch me up here, Eleanor," I said. "I'm not exactly sure what's going on."

"Charles won't sign the pre-nup," she said.

"Isn't it kind of late for a pre-nup?"

"It's not too late until I say 'I do'," she snapped. "I just got the final papers from my lawyer yesterday."

I tried another tack. "Did Charles know a pre-nup was coming?"

"Well, he should have. I mean, think about it. The guy doesn't have a pot to pee in. And he's got five kids! I only have one child."

"And you enjoy a considerably more comfortable lifestyle than Charles?" That was the best I could do in coming up with a tactful way of saying, *You're loaded and he's not.*

"Oh c'mon, Pali, I'm not kidding myself. I know I can be somewhat hard to please at times. But what I'm offering Charles is a life he's only dreamed of. All he has to do is sign the pre-nup and agree that the money's mine. It's not like I'm accusing him of anything. But if he won't sign, it's like he's saying he's only going to put up with me until he can dump me and take half of everything. It's not right."

I nodded. "Okay. How can I help?"

"Go down there and have a word with him. He'll listen to you."

I wasn't sure how much Charles was willing to listen but I agreed to give it a go. I took the elevator down to the first floor.

I knocked and Charles let me in. He said nothing. His room turned out to be a 'standard' room with a 'garden' view; the cheapest accommodation in the entire hotel.

"You know why I'm here?" I said.

"I've got a good idea."

"Well, why not just sign it?"

He stared out the window. The view was mostly parking lot. Only a thin strip of lawn with a single plumeria tree at the far edge stood between Charles' window and a half-acre of rental cars baking in the sun. Hardly a 'garden view'.

"I don't mean to be petty," he said. "But put yourself in my shoes. You've met the woman. She talks a blue streak and most of it is self-centered prattle. She's rude to waitresses and she pitches a royal fit if she has to wait for anything. My life with her will be financially comfortable but emotionally taxing. I shouldn't have to sign away my rights. To be frank, there's no way I'd marry her if she didn't have money."

I stared at him. He probably thought I was judging his candor, but instead I was indulging in a bit of my own mental self-centered prattle. Is this what money does to people? Would my father's millions turn me into an 'emotionally taxing' woman? Would Hatch resent being a 'kept man'? Maybe on some level I already knew the answers and that's why I hadn't mentioned my inheritance to anyone.

"Charles, I think you have a decision to make. You can live the high life with a demanding woman, knowing that if the marriage ends you'll get nothing. Or, you can walk away from it all right now. It's one-hundred percent up to you."

"What would you do?" he said.

"It's not for me to say. It's a tough decision."

That was a complete lie. I'd never walk away from Eleanor's money.

I'd run.

13

At dinnertime I called Hatch at the fire station and gave him an abbreviated version of how my day had gone. I started off by saying it looked like the wedding I had scheduled for the Fourth of July might fizzle. He murmured a few words of consolation. I followed up by telling him someone had dropped off a baby at Farrah's store.

"She's babysitting?" he said.

"Not exactly. The mother left the kid at the store and it doesn't sound like she's coming back."

"Did Farrah meet the mother?"

"Nope. The baby was there when she came down to open the store."

"She should have brought the kid here to the station. We can take abandoned newborns, no questions asked. And there's no blow-back on the mother for abandonment or anything."

"Well, the mother didn't do that. She left him at Farrah's."

"Has Farrah called the cops?"

"No. She's staying up here with me and Steve while she figures out what to do."

"There's nothing to figure out," he said. "She's got to report an abandoned baby. If she doesn't, she's breaking all kinds of laws—child endangerment, custodial interference, you name it."

"Look, Hatch, the child isn't in danger. And Farrah isn't interfering with anybody's custodial rights. The mother left a note saying she wanted Farrah to have him."

"Was the note signed?"

"No, anonymous."

"Then how does Farrah know the mother even wrote the note? Maybe somebody snatched the kid and ditched it at the store to elude the police. She's got to report it."

I didn't say anything.

"Pali, this isn't the former cop in me talking. I'm speaking as a friend. You've got to get Farrah to report this. She can't play 'finders keepers' with a kid. She'll end up in jail."

I changed the subject and asked him what I should wear to the firefighter dinner on Saturday night.

"Wear a dress," he said.

"But I only have the one dress. And it's starting to look a little shabby."

"So? Buy another one."

I wanted to say I'd rather bury a chopstick in my inner ear than go shopping, but I kept quiet.

"Tell you what," he said. "I'm off tomorrow. Why don't I take you to Queen Ka'ahumanu Center and we'll find you a kick-ass dress? My treat."

I agreed to go.

"Is Farrah handy?" he said. "I'd like to talk to her before we hang up."

"She's trying to put a baby crib together. From the sounds of things, it isn't a good time to interrupt."

"Tell her I'll help her with it tomorrow," he said. "Right now she needs to call the Maui Sheriff's Department."

"I'll tell her."

"Crib, huh? Someday we may need a crib, you know."

The guy was nothing if not full of surprises.

**

On Friday morning my cell phone rang as I was driving to the Palace of Pain. I hoped it was Charles saying he'd thought it over and decided to go ahead and sign the pre-nup. As annoying as Eleanor could be, maybe the love of a good man would soften her up a little.

"Pali, it's Valentine Fabares."

"Hi Valentine, I wasn't expecting to hear from you so soon."

"Yes, well, probate has been scheduled for early Monday morning. Due to the circumstances, I asked for the earliest possible spot on the docket."

"What circumstances?"

"You know, a possible petition contesting the will. If we can get this probate underway, I think the disqualified heirs will encounter a somewhat steeper slope."

"Maybe Peggy and Joanie have a point. Maybe the other children should have—"

She cut me off. "Look Pali. I knew your father. I have every confidence in the veracity of both the legality of his will and the spirit behind it. Trust me, this is what he wanted. Have you ever heard of the Golden Rule?"

"Of course, 'do unto others as you would have them do unto you'."

"That's the classic version, yes. But your father practiced a more modern version of the rule. Phil always said, 'He who has the gold, rules'. Do you see my point? It's your father's money. You and Sunny are the only people he wanted to give it to. There's no way a judge could see it differently."

"But it seems—"

"See you on Monday. We're first up so I'd appreciate it if you could plan to be over here on Sunday night. Can you do that?"

"Sure."

"Great," she said. "I'll meet you at the courthouse at eight-thirty Monday morning. *Aloha.*" The line went dead and I assumed she'd hung up.

Hatch showed up at my shop later that morning. Since the Lindberg wedding was on hold, I'd spent the last hour doing a little office housekeeping and answering emails. I hadn't slept well the night before but it wasn't due to the baby crying. I'd tossed and turned wondering how I was going to tell my friends, and especially Hatch, about my upgraded financial status.

"Ready to go rock the Kasbah?" he said. "I'm thinking you should get something glittery. And tight."

I was glad I'd asked him to pick me up at my shop rather than at home. I wanted to keep Hatch away from

Farrah because, big surprise, she hadn't called the police. She had managed to get the crib assembled, though.

As if reading my mind he said, "What did the police say when Farrah called?"

"Uh, I'm not sure. I left the house really early. She wasn't up yet."

"But she called, right?"

"As far as I know." I really wanted to change the subject. "I'm thinking maybe a blue dress. I like blue."

"To go with your eyes?"

"My eyes are hazel."

"Blue, hazel, whatever," he said. "How come women call things fifty different colors and guys get along with five? Get whatever color you want as long as it's got a really short skirt." He winked at me as if he knew a comment like that would garner some major *stink eye* and I didn't let him down.

We went from store to store to store. My feet hurt and my boredom meter had clicked into the red zone. I'd never known a guy outside of Steve's social milieu who had such shopping stamina. I was about to throw up my hands and offer to attend the dinner naked when I spied a slinky blue number with a soft draped neckline and a slit up the leg that left almost nothing to the imagination.

"But it's long," said Hatch.

"Give me a minute," I said heading to the dressing room. "I'll come out and if you hate it, I'll put it back. No argument."

I slipped on the cool shimmery dress and turned to look at myself in the mirror. The black *rubba slippas* on my feet didn't do it justice, but the color and drape of the dress hugging my body was amazing.

"Ta-dah," I said as I stepped out into the main area of the store.

Hatch stared. I twirled around to give him the full vision of the above-the-knee slit.

"Wow. I never thought long could be more sexy than short," he said.

"Common mistake," I said. "I have to explain it to brides all the time."

Hatch bought me the dress. On the way back to Pa'ia I couldn't believe how excited I felt about going to the fireman dinner at the Grand Wailea in my fancy new dress. Maybe my being Miss Richie Rich would turn out to be fun after all.

***

When I went into my shop the message light was blinking. I called the voicemail number.

"Pali, this is Charles Lindberg. I'm sorry, but I just can't do it. I can't spend the rest of my life with someone who's constantly lording her money over me. I told Eleanor my decision and now I'm leaving for home. If I owe you anything for your trouble, give me a call." He left a number with a mainland area code.

I watched in my mind's eye as my bubble of joy about becoming a rich heiress floated up, up, and away before bursting with a tiny *pop*.

14

That night I modeled my new dress for Steve and Farrah. Steve gave me a thumbs-up and Farrah—whose entire wardrobe consists of *mu'u mu'us* and caftans—declared the style and color divine. When I told her I planned to wear my new pearl amulet with it she beamed.

"But honey, since we're talking accessories," Steve said. "We've got to do *something* about those shoes."

I looked down at my 'good' sandals. They were black leather with inch-and-a-half rundown heels. "No good?"

"Are you planning to run a half-marathon between the salad and soup courses? Because those things look positively *athletic*."

"I'm not into 'do me' shoes, Steve."

"I get that, but c'mon. All you need is to take it up a notch. Maybe a lighter color, like bone or ivory, with a little bit higher heel. Let me take you shoe shopping tomorrow."

I groaned. "I'm not sure I can survive the mall two days in a row."

"Oh, get over yourself," he said. "Aren't you always telling bridesmaids it's their duty to suffer for their friend's big day? Haven't you convinced countless girls to wear the most god-awful get-ups in the name of love and friendship?"

I nodded. It was Hatch's first firefighter banquet. A little suffering was probably in order.

***

I woke up on Saturday feeling conflicted. I looked forward to my date with Hatch, but not on any level was I looking forward to three hours of tromping through the mall with Steve.

"Maybe I could borrow some shoes," I said to him over breakfast. "You've got a few drag queen friends. Maybe they'd loan me something."

"Sure, if you wear a size fifteen," he said. "Suck it up, honey, we're going sole searching. I promise I'll bless the first decent pair you find."

It sounded like a concession, but I knew Steve well enough to know his notion of 'decent' and mine were worlds apart.

Before we left for the mall I begged Farrah one more time to call the authorities and report the baby. I still hadn't heard from Sifu Doug's brother, James, and I wondered if he'd decided he didn't want to get involved.

"Hatch is coming here to pick me up tonight," I said. "He's going to grill you with his 'truth stare' and you're going to go down in flames."

"Chill," she said. "I've got a plan. I just need a little more time." She looked down at the baby asleep in her arms. When she looked up, her face was tight with resolve. "I can't let them take him. I just can't."

"Then why haven't you named him?" I said. "I'm not exactly buying that Libra in retrograde thing."

Farrah's expression relaxed. "I haven't named him because I don't have my computer hooked up yet."

"You need a *computer* to name this baby? Don't even tell me you're planning on calling him 'Google' or 'Yahoo' or whatever. That'd be criminal." I'm sure I sounded way more cranky than it called for, but since I'd been saddled with a ludicrous name I felt I had the right to weigh in.

"No," said Farrah. "I'm not searching for a geek name. I need my computer to look up his Hawaiian name. In English his name would be 'Moses' but I don't want to call him that. I need to find out the Hawaiian spelling."

"Hang on. I've got a Hawaiian dictionary around here somewhere." I rummaged through my bookshelf and came up with a yellowed copy of "The Pocket Hawaiian Dictionary," by Pukui, Elbert and Mo'okini. The blurb on the cover promised Hawaiian spellings for popular names. I flipped to the name section and found the 'M's.'

"It's *Moke*," I said. "The Hawaiian version of Moses is *Moke*."

"That's so perfect," said Farrah. She looked down at the baby's sleeping face and whispered, "*Aloha*, little *Moke. E komo mai* to your new life. Your new mama loves you with her whole heart."

It would've brought a tear to my eye but I'd already begun steeling myself to go shoe shopping.

***

As Steve pulled into a parking spot at the mall my cell began playing Mendelssohn's wedding march. That ring meant someone was calling on the 'Let's Get Maui'd' line. I checked the caller ID. I didn't recognize the number but it was an '808' area code which meant Hawaii.

"*Aloha*, this is Pali Moon," I said. I used to answer, *Pali Moon, Let's Get Maui'd*, but it was often misinterpreted.

"Hello, Pali. It's Joanie Bush, Phil Wilkerson's former wife. Do you remember me?"

"Of course. What can I do for you?"

"I got your number off the Internet. So it seems you're a wedding planner?"

"I am." I could hardly imagine the woman who'd been so nasty at the reading of my father's will would want me to coordinate a wedding for her, but maybe she'd called to apologize.

"That's pretty funny," she said.

"Oh?"

"Yeah, your dad should've kept you on retainer. I mean, think of the money he would've saved."

Had she called simply to heckle me?

"What can I do for you, Joanie?" I shot an apologetic look at Steve, who was drumming his fingers on the steering wheel.

"In this situation, it's more what I'm doing for *you*."

"Have you talked Peggy out of contesting the will?"

"Peggy's not one to be talked out of anything, I'm afraid."

"Joanie, I'm kind of busy right now. Can I call you back?"

"No can do. I'm heading off to the mainland today. Even though Phil totally screwed my kids out of what was rightfully theirs, I feel bad for you. I have some information I'm sure you'll want to know."

Steve tapped the face of his watch.

"I'm sorry, Joanie," I said. "But I'm in kind of hurry."

"Look," said Joanie. "I don't know what you've been told about your mother's death, but I'll bet it's a lie."

"I haven't been told much of anything." I felt my cheeks start to feel hot.

"Well, I'm willing to tell you the truth. Unless, of course, you don't care."

"I care very much."

By now Steve had plopped his head back on the head rest and closed his eyes. I felt trapped between hearing what Joanie had to say and continuing to rudely ignore Steve.

"I'm afraid I really can't talk right now," I said.

"That's fine with me," said Joanie. "Because I'm only willing to tell you about this face-to-face. I've got a flight to Honolulu in half-an-hour. Then I've got a short layover before I leave for the mainland at four. If you're interested in hearing what happened to your mother, meet me at the Honolulu airport."

"I'm not sure if I can…" I let it trail off.

"It's up to you. But right now I'm feeling generous. Once I get back home, who knows?"

"Okay, I'll come. I'll try to get the next flight over."

"I'll wait near the Hawaiian Airlines ticket counter. If you don't get there before I have to leave I'm not willing to wait."

We signed off and I turned to Steve.

"Let me guess," he said. "No shoes, Sherlock?"

"Looks like it."

"But what about the fireman dinner tonight? Your new dress? What about Hatch?"

"I'm only going to Honolulu. I'll get a turnaround flight and be back in plenty of time for the banquet."

"Wearing butt-ugly shoes," said Steve. "What's in Honolulu?"

"One of my dad's ex-wives is willing to tell me how my mom died. But she'll only talk to me in person so I have to meet her at the airport. If I can get on the next flight, I can hear her out and be back in a couple of hours."

"This is nuts, Pali. It's already almost one o'clock."

"I know. But I can make it work."

"And what was that about someone contesting a will?"

"Drive me to the airport and I'll tell you."

I gave him the same TV Guide version of the reading of my father's will that I'd given Hatch and Farrah. As far as my inheritance, I said my dad had left me a little money but I'd have to wait until after probate before I'd see any of it.

***

"Peep toe," Steve said as we turned onto the road that circles Kahului Airport.

"What'd you say?"

"Peep toe. That's the kind of shoes I had in mind to go with your new dress."

Steve dropped me off and I bought a ticket for the two-thirty flight with a return flight at four. It'd be tight, since it took a little over a half-hour to get from Kahului to Honolulu, but I knew I could do it.

I went through security and called Hatch. He wasn't happy with my plans.

"You want me to pick you up at the airport at four-forty-five? It'll take half-an-hour to drive back to your place and then almost another hour to get down to Wailea and get parked and everything. I don't want to be late."

"Okay, how about this: I won't go home after you pick me up. If you'll go up to my house right now and pick up my dress and shoes I can change in the airport bathroom. Then we'll have plenty of time to get down to Wailea."

His silence spoke volumes—no, an entire library—of irritation. "Pali, I know how important knowing what happened to your mom is to you. But this banquet is really important to me, too."

"Have a little faith. I'll be there."

15

Joanie Bush looked even more painted and blousy than she had on Wednesday at the attorney's office. She'd teased her hair into a towering inferno of spiky blond clumps and her talon-like nails had been re-lacquered with black nail polish with a diagonal silver racing stripe on each one. Her clingy black and white traveler knit outfit made her look downright upholstered.

She was sitting in a row of chairs by the windows. As I approached, she got up and glanced around the terminal as if checking for someone tailing her.

"Let's not talk here," she hissed. "Is there a coffee shop or somewhere where we can be alone?"

"Why don't we go outside by the lei stands? They have benches out there."

"Can I smoke?"

"I don't know. I suppose you can until they yell at you."

We went outside and walked through the parking lot to the lei stand area. We found an empty bench and as soon as we sat down Joanie rummaged through her enormous satchel and brought out a long brown cigarette.

"Want one?" she said.

I shook my head. "Never got into that."

"Well, you might consider starting after you hear what I have to say."

"Joanie, I appreciate you taking time to meet me like this, but I can do without the drama."

"Sweetie, Phil was all about drama. He lived his entire life playing to an audience."

"Tell me about my mom."

"Okay, so of course I never knew her. She'd been dead almost seven years when I met Phil. He was still married to what's-her-name, Rita, but that marriage was going south fast. I sold real estate. In fact, I sold your dad the Honolulu property in the video. Real nice views. Totally remodeled, inside and out. Four-car garage. It had granite everywhere, Brazilian hardwood floors, and even gold-plated fixtures in the master bath."

"How does this relate to my mom?"

"Hold your horses, I'm getting to that. So anyway, right after Phil and I hooked up I realized the guy had issues. He always seemed on edge, like he was waiting for the other shoe to drop. I asked him about it again and again but he claimed it was just the stress of running the cable company. Back in those days, cable was cut-throat. But Phil had friends in high places. His family back in Oregon had *beaucoup* bucks and since he was now their only son they didn't mind throwing a little cash his way when he needed it."

"He was the only one left because his brother had committed suicide," I said. I'd remembered that from Phil's video.

"Yeah, after Vietnam. Phil said his brother was messed up in the head."

I looked up. The sun was still high in the sky but at this rate I'd need to catch my flight home before I learned anything of value.

"Joanie, I'm sorry to rush you, but doesn't your flight leave at four o'clock?"

"Yeah, right. Well, here it is. Your mom didn't die of natural causes. And it wasn't an accident, either."

I was half-expecting something like that, but still I felt the blood rush to my ears. I could hear a faint *thud, thud, thud* in my left ear.

"How did she die?"

"Before we get to that, let me say I got this on good authority. This isn't just idle gossip."

I shot her a puzzled look.

"Phil told me this himself. He said he didn't abandon your mom. He kept in touch. That's why when he found out about her getting killed he took it real hard."

"Was he… I mean, did he have anything to do it?"

"No way. He said he loved her 'like a rock.' You know, like that old Paul Simon song, 'Love Me Like a Rock'? He never got over what happened."

"What did happen?"

"He told me a jealous guy who had a crush on her came in and killed her one night after she'd snubbed him. Phil said the guy was probably hopped up on something. Those Kaua'i hippies were always smokin' weed and dropping acid and stuff like that."

"But Auntie Mana said she'd died of a cerebral hemorrhage."

"Well, according to your father, the guy hit her over the head with a piece of wood or something. She got a bad concussion that made her brain bleed. Seems she died before she got to the hospital."

Images of my mother cowering under the blows of a crazed attacker flashed before me. "Did they catch the guy?"

"No. According to Phil, he totally got away with it."

"If my dad loved my mom so much why didn't he demand justice for her?"

"He said he wanted to, but there was a big cover-up. And that's why he was nervous all the time after he moved back to Hawaii. He said he thought the family involved in the cover-up might come after him."

"Why?"

"Because they knew he knew."

Joanie flipped her cigarette to the ground and stubbed it out with the toe of a very pointy black patent pump. Steve would've no doubt gushed over those shoes. I stealthily slid my foot next to hers to check if they'd fit. Nope, her feet were at least two sizes too big. Not that I'd expect her to trade her Rodeo Drive pumps for my ABC Store flip-flops, but it wouldn't hurt to ask.

"You're saying my mom was murdered," I said by way of a wrap up.

"I'm afraid so. And your dad never got over it. I guess that's why he left you all that dough. It's totally unfair to my kids, but I guess I'll let sleeping dogs lie." She shook her head. "Excuse me for being honest, but your dad was a total dog. Half the crap that came out of his mouth was lies."

"But he never told you who he thought killed my mom?"

"No. He said the guy was from an important family, and if he told me then I'd be in danger too. He said the killer's old man had lots of clout and lots of dough."

I thanked her for meeting with me and we got up and retraced our steps through the parking lot. When we crossed the busy airport road, she veered left toward the overseas terminal and I headed right to the interisland gates.

I took out my cellphone and checked the time. My flight to Maui left in twenty minutes.

***

My flight was delayed. First, they said it would be fifteen minutes. Then, after fifteen minutes they said there was a mechanical problem and they were waiting for a mechanic to check it out. By the time the next flight had boarded, they'd cancelled my flight.

"I've got to get to Maui," I told the gate agent. "I've got an urgent appointment."

"Our next flight is at six-forty-five," she said. "But I'm afraid it's oversold. We can probably get you on the seven-ten. It'll get you into Kahului around seven-forty-five."

The banquet began with cocktails at six and then dinner at seven.

I called Hatch and told him I couldn't make it.

"What the hell?" he shouted. "You promised me, Pali. Now I'm going to be the only guy without a date. I'm gonna look like a frickin' loser." I assumed he'd be disappointed, but what did the yelling accomplish? Then

I remembered that guys like Hatch don't do sadness; they do anger. I'd seen it plenty of times in martial arts. A guy loses a fight in a competition. He bows to his opponent like he's supposed to, and then he goes out to his car and kicks in the door panel.

"I sorry. I was really looking forward to it."

"Then why'd you go running off to Honolulu at the last minute?"

"Hatch, it's complicated. I had to hear what my dad's ex-wife had to say."

"I went and got someone to cover my shift today so I could go to this thing. And now if I don't show up everyone will know I'm just sitting home with my finger in my…. And I'm up for that award, too."

"What award?"

"What does it matter? The point is, now I can't go."

"Hatch, I said I was sorry." A beat went by and I said, "Okay, I've got an idea. How about you invite Farrah? I'm sure she'll go. She'd do anything for you."

"You think? But she won't be able to fit in your new dress."

"I think you're gonna have to be okay with a date wearing a caftan."

"But I was really looking forward to seeing you in that dress."

"I'd love to be there. But I can't."

"I forgot to ask about your mom," he said. "What'd you find out?"

I looked around and everyone in the gate area was glaring at me. Nobody likes a waiting room blabbermouth who pollutes the air with their personal drama. "I'd rather not talk about it right now. Have fun tonight."

"I'll try. But you owe me one."

"I know."

We hung up and I stared out the window. I felt bad about missing Hatch's banquet, but maybe it was for the best. How could I eat, drink and make merry when I'd just learned my mother had been bludgeoned to death?

16

As I slumped in my seat at the interisland terminal it occurred to me I was already halfway to Kaua'i. I got out my cell phone and the business card Sunny had given me.

"*Aloha*," she said.

"*Aloha*, Sunny. It's me Pali."

"Hey, good to hear from you. Are you here on Kaua'i?"

"Not yet. But I'm in Honolulu and I thought if you wouldn't mind I'd come over a day early."

"Sounds great. I'll have my driver pick you up at the airport."

"That's okay. I can rent a car," I said.

"No, no, totally unnecessary. Timo will be glad to have a reason to get out of here."

I turned in my Kahului return ticket and paid the difference for the flight to Lihue. Then I called Sunny to let her know when I'd be landing. "Great. When you get here, go outside and keep an eye out for a white Range Rover."

By the time I made it off the plane and through the Lihue terminal it'd been nearly half an hour beyond the time I'd given Sunny. I rushed outside and spotted a big

Range Rover slowly driving along the airport circle road. I waved and Sunny's driver, Timo, pulled over. He jumped out and dashed around the car to open the back door.

"Can I sit up front with you?" I said. I thought it'd feel weird to sit in the back all by myself. And I wanted to talk to the guy and see if he had anything to say about working for my father.

Timo scowled and slammed the door. I climbed into the passenger seat and we headed out. The guy was no chatterbox. In fact, he answered even basic 'icebreaker' questions with a 'dunno' or a shrug.

We drove up the highway to Kapa'a and then just beyond town, Timo turned inland, or *mauka*.

"Phil Wilkerson didn't live on the ocean?" I said.

"No," he said. He looked over at me and must've realized I was growing weary of his sullen responses because he went on. "He had other places that were on the water. But here he liked the peace and quiet. You'll see."

We turned at a single-lane road with a metal gate across it. Timo used a remote to open the gate and soon the bumpy dirt road became just two dirt ruts winding through overgrown vegetation. The car jostled up and down at such a pitch I had to grip the armrest to keep from whacking my head on the side window.

"Wow, this is pretty secluded," I said. Outside, the car was traveling through what I would have described as 'jungle.' Thick green foliage brushed against the sides of the car, and it was hard to see more than ten feet ahead.

"Yeah. Like I tell you, Mr. Phil liked privacy."

When we finally came within view of the house it was like being in an airplane popping out of the clouds into bright sunshine. We went from deep green overgrowth to a wide open meadow of manicured lawn. A steep mountain jutted up from behind the house.

"This is like a fairy tale," I said. The large house was plantation-style, with a shallow sloping gabled roof and a covered *lanai*, or what mainlanders call a 'porch', that wrapped completely around. The main floor of the house was raised about five feet off the ground and there were wide steps leading up to the main level.

"Do you know the name of that mountain?" I said. I was expecting Timo to toss me another 'dunno' but he surprised me.

"That there is Sleeping Giant," he said pointing to the main peak. "In Hawaiian, we call it *Nounou*. The legend is that a giant drank too much at a party. He laid down to take a nap and he never got up. See his hands on his belly?"

"Wow. Like I said, this place reminds me of a fairy tale."

Sunny came out on the *lanai* to greet us. She waved as if welcoming home a long lost relative. Then it hit me—she was my step-mother. It felt weird to claim her as a family member, and especially weird that a woman five years younger than me would qualify for the 'mother' category.

"Pali, *e komo mai* to my humble home," she said as I got out. *Humble?* Hardly.

"Timo, please bring up Pali's luggage," she said gesturing for me to join her.

"I don't have any luggage, Sunny," I said. "I got called to Honolulu unexpectedly. I may need to go to Kapa'a to pick up a few things before court on Monday."

"Nonsense," she said. "I've got everything you'll need right here. Fresh toothbrush, shampoo and conditioner, you name it. And you can borrow a nightshirt and even a change of underwear if you'd like. We're about the same size."

Oh great. Now I'd be literally getting into my step-mother's pants. Why had I thought coming over here on the fly was a good idea?

Timo drove off to who knows where to park the car. Sunny laid a hand on my shoulder. "Oh good news," she said. "Peggy called and said she's willing to talk about not contesting the will."

The ex-wives keep in touch? How many women do that?

Sunny went on, "But she reminded me that she's got four years to think about it."

"Four years?"

"Yeah, so even if the judge says the probate is a go, anyone can come in later and mess it up." She nodded to a grouping of chairs on the *lanai*. "You want to sit out here or go inside?"

"Out here's good." I said. "So just anybody can contest it?"

"No, silly. They have to be an heir."

Something about her patronizing tone made me clench my right hand. I decided to forgo the small talk and cut to the chase. "Sunny, I met with Joanie at the

Honolulu airport and she told me my mother had been murdered."

"What?"

"Yeah, she said my dad told her about it. She said Phil told her a jealous guy killed her and he got away with it because he was from a prominent family." I stared at Sunny, watching her eyes to see whether I could pick up if she'd heard the same story from Phil.

"Wow, that's crazy," she said. "Do you believe her?"

"Why would she lie?"

"Who knows? Maybe because she's still pissed that Phil left you the money. You know, she can be nasty."

"True. But I always thought there was something fishy about how my mother died. My Auntie Mana used to talk about my mom all the time, but she never once said anything about how she died."

"The locals here are like that. They don't talk much about death and dying."

"But if she died in a car wreck or from an illness or something, why not just say it? It's not like I wanted gruesome details."

"Maybe you should ask her."

"Auntie Mana died right after I finished college." It occurred to me that Phil would have known that if he'd been following me like he claimed in his video.

"You know, when you're talking prominent families on Kaua'i, it's hard to beat the Chestertons," said Sunny. "Peggy's father was mayor of the island in the eighties and nineties. And her brother AJ was kind of a stoner. Phil said AJ straightened up later, and I guess now he's big in resort development. But don't believe everything you hear. Joanie and Peggy never liked each other and one's always bad-mouthing the other one. Maybe Joanie just told you that out of spite."

"Could be."

"You know, Phil and Joanie had a knock-down, drag-out divorce. And partly it was because he stayed tight with the Chestertons his whole life. I was cool with it, and I'm sure the other wives were too. I mean, the Chesterton name opens doors around here. But Joanie never understood why Phil kept toadying up to his ex-in-laws."

"Do you think what Joanie told me was a lie?"

"What do you think?"

In the silence that followed, I looked out from my comfortable perch on the _lanai_. The light was beginning to fade, but the view was still astounding. The house was surrounded by a wide lawn bordered by a wall of palms, wide-leaf Hawaiian philodendron, _ti_ plants and brilliant red and yellow crotons.

"It's beautiful here," I said.

"Yeah, this house was your father's favorite. He died right where you're sitting."

I turned to her, speechless.

Sunny shrugged. "One minute he was here and the next he wasn't. It was a real crappy day, for sure."

Again we lapsed into silence.

Sunny stood up. "Let me get you something to drink." She went inside and came out with a pitcher and two wine glasses. "I call this 'island sangria'," she said. She held up the pitcher. Her island sangria was sweet white wine infused with chunks of orange, papaya and pineapple. She poured me a glass. I was thirsty and the sweet wine went down easy. By my second glass, I wasn't hearing much of what she was saying.

"I'm feeling a little sick," I said dragging myself up and out of the chair. Although I'm sure it came out more like *fella lil sock* since the wine had definitely messed with my lip/tongue coordination.

"Why don't I take you out to the *ohana*? You can take a nap before we have dinner."

The *ohana*, or guest house, was about a hundred yards from the main house. It was totally private, thanks to a tall hedge between it and the house. The driveway made a detour to the front of the *ohana* and then continued around to join up with the rutted road leading out to the highway.

Although it was only one story, the *ohana* was larger than my house in Hali'imaile. It had three bedrooms plus a spacious den, a living room, a full kitchen, two and a half baths and a sun porch. The place could've easily sheltered a family of four.

"This is gorgeous, Sunny," I said. "I'm sorry but I'm going to need the bathroom right away."

I went into the nearby powder room and barely made it to the toilet in time. It must have been something I ate. Or maybe it was drinking on an empty stomach. Whatever it was, I washed my hands and splashed some water on my face and I felt a bit better.

"Are you okay?" said Sunny when I came back out.

"I'm fine, but it's been a stressful day. If it's okay with you I think I'll skip dinner. I'm not that hungry."

"Okay. Well then, just relax. Your father loved this *ohana*," she said. "He loved to come out here to enjoy the quiet."

When she left, I plopped down on the tropical-print tapestry sofa and ran my hand across the nubby fabric. My dad had sat on that sofa, probably even slept out on it. He'd no doubt looked out the wide windows of the sun porch and gazed at Sleeping Giant Mountain. I wanted to contemplate the enormity of what I'd learned in the past four days but weariness came over me. I stretched out my legs and before I knew it I'd conked out.

17

Was the pounding in my head? No, it was coming from somewhere else. I rubbed my eyes and sat up. It was pitch black outside and someone was pounding on the door. I got up but my knees buckled and I plopped back down. I heard a voice yelling my name from the other side of the door.

I shook my head and stood up again. This time I managed to remain vertical. I unsteadily made my way across the dark room to the front door. The pounding and yelling continued. I snapped on the porch light and peered through the peep-hole. I saw the mole on Peggy Chesterton's face magnified to the size of a fist.

I opened the door a crack. "What are you doing here?"

"I came to talk to you," she said in a slurry voice. "Are you going to let me in or not?"

I pulled the door open and she lumbered inside, tossing her colossal shoulder bag on a chair before flopping down on the sofa. She looked positively wasted. I wondered how she'd managed to get through the locked gate to the property. And I wondered how much she'd had to drink.

"I hear you've been talking to Joanie," she said.

"More to the point, Joanie's been talking to me."

"Yeah, well whatever. Sunny told me Joanie gave you an earful of crap about how your mother died. You don't believe any of it, do you?"

Her eyes were so bloodshot she looked like she'd been in a brawl.

"I don't know what to believe," I said. "But it never made sense to me that she just up and died. She was only twenty-five, you know."

"No, but purple have accidents all the time." She'd said *purple*, but I figured she meant *people*. No sense in correcting her. The way she was acting, I was pretty sure she wouldn't hesitate to throw a punch.

"That's true."

"And I hear your mom was one of those hippies up at Taylor Camp. Maybe she got high and fell outta her tree house," She shot me a crooked smile.

Maybe a little smack-down wasn't such a bad idea, after all. "Joanie said a guy from a well-known island family came in one night and killed her in a jealous rage. Seems the guy was a pot-head. And afterward, his family covered it up."

"Really?" She'd lost the smile.

"From what I've heard, the Chestertons are one of the most well-known families on Kaua'i. And Sunny tells me your brother AJ was pretty fond of his *pakalolo* back in the day."

"Ha! My brother and your mother? If what you're implying wasn't so insulting it'd be funny. My brother owns a big chunk of this island and my father was the mayor here for twelve years. Do you think for one minute either one of them gave two shakes about some hippie skank on the North Shore?"

I got up and jerked the front door open. "You better leave." My hands were shaking and I felt like throwing up.

She came over and stopped in the doorway. She had an odor coming off her that reminded me of something oozing from a hole in the ground. "I'll leave. But before you go shooting your mouth off, you need to remember who you're dealing with. My family's been on Kaua'i since before dirt. Your father used my father's pull to get where he got. If your mom got herself killed, that's too bad. But before you go 'slathering' the Chesterton name you better get your facts straight. Because around here, we don't hold grudges. We hold funerals."

I would've chuckled at her use of the word 'slather' for 'slander' but I was taking her threat seriously.

She lurched out onto the porch. She appeared even more inebriated than when she'd first come in. Before she got to the steps, she turned. "You know, your mother's death wasn't hush-hush. It was all anybody talked about for weeks."

She staggered down the steps and I slammed the door. I winced at the thought that she'd be drunk driving. I hoped she lived nearby.

I headed into Phil's den. If my mom's death had been the gist of local gossip, maybe I'd be able to find something on the computer. I hoped Phil hadn't been so obsessed with peace and quiet that he hadn't had an Internet connection installed.

The computer booted up and thankfully, Phil hadn't set it up with a password. With just a few keystrokes I found the link to the archives of *The Garden Island*, the local Kaua'i newspaper. I went to the search box and typed in 'Hanalei murder 1981.' I gripped my shaking hands into fists while the computer took a second to search. But when the results came up, nothing it listed was over five years old. I tried other keywords but still nothing.

The next day was Sunday, so I'd have to stop by the newspaper office on Monday after probate court. I'd also drop by the police station and see if I could bluff my way into getting my hands on the police report. I'd try invoking the Freedom of Information Act. I wasn't exactly sure what the FIA covered or who could use it to get what, but I thought it sounded good.

I logged off the computer and started rummaging through the furniture in the den. The big mahogany desk was first. There were three drawers on each side with a pencil drawer in the middle. The files in the bottom drawers were mostly copies of paid bills and bank statements. I didn't care about any of that. I already knew my dad was rich. I wanted to see if he'd kept any mementos from his days at Taylor Camp.

In a far corner of the pencil drawer I found a tattered envelope so worn it felt more like fabric than paper. Inside was an old black and white photograph; the kind with the date printed in the margin of the white scalloped edge. The date was August 15, 1976—two months after I'd been born. The image was a little blurry but it still made me shiver. It showed three people, a woman in the middle and two men on either side. Looking at the woman's face was like looking in a mirror. It had to be my mother. I'd seen photos in Auntie Mana's scrapbooks, but I'd never noticed before how much I resembled her.

The men on either side seemed to be about the same age or maybe a few years apart. One had a full beard and a big smile; the other guy squinted at the camera as if he'd rather be somewhere else. The squinter looked vaguely familiar. High forehead, prominent nose. Perhaps it was Phil in earlier times? It was hard to tell.

I continued rifling through drawers and shelves but didn't find anything else that intrigued me. I went back to the photo. Who was the other guy? Probably a Taylor Camp friend.

I was dead tired, but I didn't want to go into the bedroom and lie down on Phil's bed. I wondered how good it would feel to totally trash this fancy house of my father's. The man who'd abandoned the mother of his child. The guy who'd left my mother to fend for herself among a tribe of weed smokers and dopers. When one of those dopers, most probably A J Chesterton, got hopped up one night and viciously attacked her, where was Philip J. Wilkerson the Third? Nowhere to be found. From where I was sitting, my father was as guilty of my mother's murder as if he'd killed her himself.

I was sick, exhausted, and dizzy. I went into the living room and dived onto the sofa.

***

I was pretty sure my cell phone was ringing. I opened one eye, then the other. Light streamed through the living room windows. I went through the whole *Where am I? What day is this?* routine before I was awake enough to answer it.

"Pali, how's it going?" It was Farrah.

"Not one of my better mornings," I said with a voice that sounded like I'd survived a near-strangulation.

She laughed. "Sorry to hassle you, but I wanted to see how you were doing. You missed a real groovy party last night. Did you hear? Hatch was up for Rookie of the Year and he won! Far out, right? He's been strutting around here like a Chinese peacock."

I heard Hatch's laugh in the background.

"Where are you?" I said.

"We're up here at the house. I promised him a big breakfast for taking me last night."

I wasn't even going to ask for clarification on *that* one.

"Farrah, I'm sorry but I'm feeling kind of sick. Can I call you back in a little while?"

"Don't you want to talk to Hatch?"

"Sure, put him on."

"Hey," he said.

"Hey," I said. "Congratulations on being Rookie of the Year."

"Yeah, *mahalo*. The dinner turned out to be pretty great. So what's going on with you?"

"It's been crazy. My dad's ex-wife told me my mother hadn't died of natural causes. She said my mom was murdered. And now I've found a picture of her here at Phil's house."

"Whoa. Do you believe her? Uh-oh, sorry, but I gotta run. I just got handed a huge plate of French toast with my name on it."

In the background I heard Farrah say. "Which name would that be? 'Hatch Decker'? or 'Maui Fire Rookie of the Year'?"

They both laughed and Hatch hurriedly said his good-byes and hung up.

I snapped the phone shut. A flash of anger shot through me. Why couldn't I get anyone else to care about this as much as I did? And then it hit me. There were only two people on this earth who'd ever care as much, and I was one of them.

I thought of my little brother running down the beach calling for his mom. Someone had gotten away with her murder and left us orphans. I picked up the black and white photo and scrutinized my mother's face. It'd been thirty years but the killer still had a debt to pay.

And if it took thirty more, I wouldn't rest until I'd collected on that debt.

18

Sunny called a few minutes later and invited me to breakfast. My stomach was still roiling, but I needed to eat something. As I made my way over to the main house I noticed Peggy had 'gone off the rails' when she left the night before. There were deep tire ruts in the lawn where she'd failed to stay on the road.

Sunny met me at the door with a glass of guava juice. I love guava and started to drink it but stopped after one gulp. It tasted so sweet it nearly gagged me. I carried the glass with me to the kitchen and set it on the counter.

"How'd you sleep?" she asked.

"Well, after Peggy left—"

"Oh no, did Peggy come over and bother you? I told her Joanie was just being a bitch. But I thought Peggy should know what she'd told you. It's best to have stuff like that out in the open, don't you think?"

"She acted drunk. Was Peggy drunk when she talked to you?"

"Oh, Phil told me Peggy always had a drinking problem. That's why he finally called it quits. They were married for a long time, but enough's enough. She claims she's sober now, but it doesn't look like it."

Sunny had laid out a huge fruit plate with pineapple, mango, papaya, and bananas all artfully arranged. It looked like something I'd order for a bridal brunch party. There was also a plate of muffins and a pitcher of the guava juice. I steered clear of the juice but helped myself to a muffin and a large portion of fruit.

I pulled the photo from my purse and showed it to Sunny. She smiled when she recognized who was in it. "That's Phil," she said pointing to the scowling man.

"And who's the other guy?"

"Um, I'm pretty sure that's his brother, Robert."

"The one who killed himself?"

"Yeah." She turned away.

"What is it?"

"Oh, nothing," she said. "Where'd you get that picture?"

I told her about finding it in his desk. She got up and scraped the leftover fruit into the garbage. If I'd had leftover fruit I would've put it in a plastic container in the refrigerator.

She sighed and sat down. "I guess I should tell you. With Joanie mouthing off and Peggy falling off the wagon, it's bound to come out sooner or later. Let's go sit on the *lanai*. It's nicer out there."

We went outside.

"This is not a happy story, Pali. But you deserve to know the whole story."

She'd known all along? Oh well, better late than never.

"Phil told me what happened was an accident. A really sad accident."

I felt a tightness in my neck and had to roll my shoulders to get the kinks out. I still felt somewhat sick to my stomach so I hoped Sunny's story wouldn't send me fleeing to the bathroom again.

"Your father didn't just up and leave your mother. He cared about her a lot, but he'd run out of money. He asked his parents for help, but instead they demanded he come home to Oregon and go to college. He said he promised himself he'd come back to Kaua'i one day, but he didn't think it was fair to ask your mom to wait for him."

She looked at me as if checking if I was buying what she was selling. I did my best to keep a neutral face.

"Anyway, he said a few years after he was out of the picture Peggy's brother, AJ, tried to put the moves on your mom. She was already hooking up with another guy, but AJ was used to getting his way and wouldn't take 'no' for an answer. After all, his dad was the chief of police and all."

"Oh that's right. Peggy's dad was the police chief before he became mayor."

"Yeah, so anyway, one night AJ went all crazy and came after your mom's new lover with a bat. From what Phil told me, your mom tried to break it up. She got between the two guys. Nobody was exactly sure what happened, but she got hit on the head and she later died. So you see, it wasn't murder; it was just a horrible accident." Sunny stopped and took a deep breath as if recalling a tragic scene she'd rather not revisit.

"But didn't the police investigate? I mean, AJ and this other guy were fighting and my mother got *killed*."

"Think about it. AJ was the police chief's son. And besides that, according to Phil, back then there was no love lost between the cops and the hippies. Phil said even if the police had tried to investigate, nobody would've talked to them."

"So how did Phil hear all this?"

"He said he'd kept in touch with some people he'd known at Taylor Camp."

"So who was the other guy?"

"What other guy?"

"The guy my mom *died* trying to protect."

"Oh him," said Sunny. "Phil said he and your mom had a baby together. So I guess that would make him your half-brother's father."

"Uncle Robby."

"Did you know him?" she said.

"I vaguely remember him. I was five when my mom died. And now that I think about it, I never saw Uncle Robby again after Auntie Mana moved us to Maui."

I paused a moment. "But then after my dad graduated, he came back to Kaua'i and married Peggy Chesterton?"

"Yeah. Seems kind of weird, doesn't it? But he said one of the things he and Peggy had in common was they shared that tragic secret." She shook her head. "Peggy's brother and your mom. I'm sorry I was the one who had to tell you."

"I appreciate it. It answers a lot of questions."

We sat there a moment and Sunny's home phone started ringing.

"I'll let you get that," I said.

I went over to the *ohana* to use the bathroom one more time. My stomach was still doing flip-flops and Sunny's story hadn't helped. I hoped whatever it was that had made me sick would be out of my system before I had to go to court on Monday morning.

As I was walking back to the main house, my cell phone rang.

"Pali? It's Valentine. I'm afraid I have some bad news. Peggy Chesterton died this morning. It seems she was in a terrible car accident last night."

19

I started jogging toward the main house. "What? Peggy's dead? I just saw her last night."

I was taking the stairs to the *lanai* two at a time when Valentine said, "Yes, and Sunny told me she'd been to see you right before the accident."

I stopped mid-stride. "What?"

"I just spoke with Sunny and she said Peggy had come over to see you last night. She said Peggy seemed very upset about some allegations you'd made about her brother."

I looked up at the door to Sunny's but didn't take another step.

"Anyway," Valentine went on. "I'm so glad I caught up with you. I had no idea you were already here on Kaua'i. Since it appears you were the last person to see Peggy before the accident I'm sure the police will want to talk to you. My advice is to not say anything. Call me immediately. I can be there in twenty minutes."

I slowly made my way up the rest of the stairs and across the *lanai*. Through the screen door I could see Sunny in the kitchen putting the dishes away. She was humming like she hadn't a care in the world.

"Sunny," I said, coming into the house without knocking. "You heard about Peggy?"

She nodded. I detected a faint glimmer of smugness in her eyes.

"Why did you tell Valentine Fabares I'd pissed off Peggy?" I said.

"You wouldn't want me to lie, would you? And besides, that's what I told the police when they called earlier. I did you a favor by contacting Valentine. She said she'd be willing to help if you were brought in for questioning."

***

The police arrived less than ten minutes later in an unmarked car. I went to the window and watched a guy in plain clothes get out from the passenger side and then his partner, a young woman, get out from the driver side.

I went to the door and the woman spoke first. "We're looking for Pali Moon. Is that you?"

I nodded.

"I'm Detective Kiki Wong and this is my partner, Detective Dennis Akanu. We're investigating a fatal accident from last night and your name came up."

I was stunned. *Detective Wong*, really? I knew a detective on Maui named Glen Wong, but Kiki Wong didn't look anything like my Wong. Although they were both clearly of Asian descent, Kiki was tiny, maybe ninety pounds. She was only about five two, maybe five three. Glen Wong wasn't a big man, but he was average height and pretty buff. As far as I could see, if there was a familial connection, it wasn't a close one.

I thought Kiki was dressed rather provocatively for a cop. She had on a deep V-necked black tank top with a short-sleeved blue 'cop shirt' over it. The shirt was unbuttoned and tied at her waist.

Detective Wong appeared to be the kind of gal who would act impressed with my success in martial arts and then challenge me to a fight and clean my clock. Her partner was a middle-aged local guy who looked like he should've been teaching high school math instead of investigating homicides and busting meth dealers.

I opened the screen to let them in. "I really don't have anything to say. I didn't even know about the accident until this morning."

Sunny came out of the kitchen. "*Aloha*, Kiki. Good to see you again, although once again it's under sad circumstances."

Detective Kiki Wong gave Sunny a tight smile. "Yes, Mrs. Wilkerson. Sad circumstances are an unfortunate part of the job."

She turned to me. "We got a tip that Mrs. Margaret Chesterton was out here last night talking to you before the accident."

I considered what Valentine had said about saying nothing, but then decided that nipping this in the bud would be the better option. "Yes, Peggy came over last night totally '*ona*, you know, drunk. She and I chatted for a couple of minutes and then she left."

Both detectives gave me the cop squint. Then Wong went on, "So you allowed an intoxicated woman to get in her car and drive away?"

"I, uh." I tried to come up with a good excuse, and Valentine's words echoed. "You know, I don't think I want to talk about this anymore without my lawyer present."

I looked over at Sunny. She shrugged. Then she leaned in and whispered, "You want me to get Valentine on the phone?"

"I guess you better."

***

The cops were kind enough to give me a lift to the station. The back of the cop car was like you see on TV, a slick vinyl bench seat and no door handles. Through the wire mesh separating the back from the front I could see all kinds of high-tech stuff. They had a GPS screen, an on-board computer, dash-mounted camera; the whole nine yards.

"Wow, you guys are well-equipped," I said. "The cops on Maui would love to have that much hardware."

Neither cop turned to acknowledge me.

After a few moments, Akanu said, "You ride in cop cars much on Maui?"

I decided to shut up for the rest of the trip.

They took me inside and brought me to an interview room. I've been in a few police station interview rooms before. It's not like I'm a habitual criminal or anything; it just seems I'm a person that cops like to talk to.

Valentine arrived minutes later. She and the detectives greeted each other. I felt like a dog at the pound. Like I hadn't done anything to deserve this, but now my fate was in total strangers' hands.

"Anyone want coffee? How about some water?" Akanu played the gracious host while Wong glared with her arms crossed. Valentine established the pecking order by declining for us both. I could've gone for a Diet Pepsi but I didn't want to cross her.

"Let's start from the top," said Wong. "At what time did the victim arrive at your premises?"

Oh great. So now they were referring to Peggy Chesterton as 'the victim'. I glanced at Valentine and saw she'd picked up on it too.

"You don't have to answer that, Pali."

"We're just trying to establish a timeline, here, Ms. Fabares. Nothing more."

"My client doesn't wish to assist in establishing your timeline unless you plan to charge her with something. What difference does it make what time Mrs. Chesterton arrived?"

"Can I answer?" I said.

"No," said Valentine. "You may not."

I leaned in and whispered in her ear. "I have no idea when she got there. I was asleep on the sofa and when I woke up she was at the door. I don't wear a watch and I didn't see a clock so I can honestly say I don't know what time it was."

"My client doesn't recall what time it was," Valentine said. Not nearly as good an answer as mine.

"Okay," said Wong. "Does your client *recall* if it was light outside or dark?"

There was no way I could avoid answering that. I looked at Valentine.

"My client doesn't recall."

"Why don't you ask your client if she'd like to answer before you answer for her?"

"Because this is a waste of time. My client has no knowledge of anything regarding Mrs. Chesterton's tragic automobile accident."

"Your client has already told us that Mrs. Chesterton appeared to be impaired when she left the premises."

Valentine said, "Peggy Chesterton had a severe drinking problem when she was younger. But she'd been clean and sober for years, maybe decades. It wouldn't have taken more than a couple glasses of wine for her to appear more impaired than she probably was. But regardless, my client has no medical or police training to allow her to ascertain a person's blood alcohol content."

I was baffled by the logic, but I'd put my trust in Valentine's lawyering so I kept quiet.

"True," said Wong. "But regardless of her BAC, if she appeared impaired, she was most probably impaired."

Detective Akanu maintained a zen-like smile but his eyes bore into mine as if he was trying to fit me for glasses.

The two detectives exchanged a look and then Wong got up and left. After a half-minute of silence Akanu spoke up. "You know, all she's trying to do here is get to the bottom of this. No one's accusing anyone of anything. But when a respected citizen such as Mrs. Chesterton runs off the road and into a tree for no apparent reason, we like to find out what happened."

The guy sounded like Dr. Phil. And, like a guest on the Dr. Phil Show, I really wanted to tell him my story.

Valentine said, "Detective Akanu, I respect you're just doing your job. But I'm doing mine. My client has nothing to say."

Akanu got up and left. I turned to say something to Valentine but she pointed to the camera in the corner. I folded my hands on the table and stared at the mirror on the other side of the room. Twenty minutes later we were told we were free to go.

We walked outside and I said, "Why won't you let me tell them the truth?"

"Because they will use it against you."

"But I don't know anything."

Valentine turned on me. "Look," she said. "Don't you *ever* disregard my instructions again. I told you to say *nothing*. I'm doing my best to distance you from this. From now on, do exactly what I say. It's your only way out."

Not much of a vote of confidence.

She asked if I wanted a ride to Sunny's and I nodded.

"I don't have anything to wear to court tomorrow. Do you know of a shop in Kapa'a that's open today?"

"I'd rather you didn't leave the compound. Why don't you see if you can borrow something from your step-mother?"

We pulled out onto the highway and I said, "Do you think I had anything to do with Peggy Chesterton's death?"

"I don't know and I don't want to know," she said.

Nope, not much of a vote of confidence at all.

***

When we got to Sunny's I called Farrah. "I'm sorry we didn't get to talk very long this morning. I didn't get a chance to ask you how things are going with Moke."

"Oh, Moke's great. In fact, in a few minutes Hatch is taking us all down to the beach. We're gonna dip his little feet in the ocean for the very first time. I wish you could be here."

What? Hatch was helping Farrah bond with Moke? He'd done a complete about-face since Friday when he'd been ranting about child endangerment and kidnapping.

"Oops. Sorry Pali, but I've gotta run," she said. "Hatch is out there blowing the horn and I still have to pack the diaper bag. I tell ya, Pali, this mother stuff isn't for wusses." She trilled an *aloha* and hung up.

20

Sunny buzzed Valentine through the gate but I asked to be dropped off at the *ohana* rather than the main house. I wasn't in the mood to give Sunny a play-by-play of what'd happened at the police station. I was afraid she'd enjoy it too much. Instead, I went into the guest house and crashed on the sofa. I awoke to the phone ringing. It was Sunny, asking me if I'd like to join her for dinner. I didn't feel hungry, but I was going to have to hit her up for something to wear to court so I accepted.

"I'm not a great cook," she said as I came in. "But your dad didn't mind. We ate out a lot and he was mostly a steak and rice guy. He bought himself a fancy grill and got a rice cooker for me and we were good to go."

She seemed awfully chipper under the circumstances. I told her about Valentine not allowing me to defend myself. I also told her about Valentine's seeming lack of faith in my innocence.

"Oh, don't worry about it," she said. "Valentine's a worry wart. Goes with the territory, I guess. She used to drive your father nuts with her nit-picking and her 'sign this' and 'initial that.' When we got married and he told her he wanted to sign everything over to me as community property I thought she'd have a heart attack. She didn't want him to leave me a dime."

I asked if she'd mind loaning me something to wear to court and she invited me into the master bedroom. I felt uncomfortable looking at the king-size bed set against the wall. It was much too intimate a reminder of her relationship with my father.

She went into a walk-in closet and came out with a beautifully-tailored deep green linen sheath. "How about this? It will go great with your eyes."

"Oh, wow. That's really nice. But what will you wear?"

She flicked a finger for me to join her in the closet. The room was as nearly as big as her kitchen, with fancy shelving and shoe racks. It even had a center island with drawers and a granite top. I stood slack-jawed, staring at row upon row of dresses, blouses, skirts, and pants. All were grouped by color. Her shoe collection took up an entire wall.

"I think I'll be able to find something. Now, how about shoes?" She looked down at my *rubba slippas*. "What are you? About a seven?"

I nodded. She handed me a pair of taupe-colored sandals that probably cost more than the Kelly Blue Book on my car.

"*Mahalo*. I'll get this dress cleaned and send it back."

"Oh puh-leeze. Keep it. Since Phil bought me all this, half of it is yours now anyway." She laughed but it made me almost as uncomfortable as staring at the bed.

We went back into the kitchen. She pulled some salad makings out of the refrigerator and asked if I'd do the honors.

"You never answered my question about how long you two were married before my father died," I said.

"I know. I guess I'm a little touchy about it. See, I took care of your dad for nearly two years before we got married. Then—' She stopped and I looked up from making the salad. She was biting her lip and blinking back tears. It was the first time I'd seen her show any emotion over the death of my father.

"I'm sorry. You don't have to talk about this if you don't want to," I said.

"No, it's fine. I can't believe it still gets to me. We both knew what was going to happen. It wasn't like it was a shock or anything."

"But still, it's hard," I said.

"Yeah. I feel bad that you never got to know him. He was one in a million."

"Sounds like it. But I've got to say, it's hard for me to bring up good feelings about him. And now that I know he knew my mom had been killed and he never came for me… Well, all I can say is I'm lucky Auntie Mana stepped up when she did. My brother and I had nobody."

"Your father cared for you in the only way he knew how. But he had to keep a low profile."

I stared at her. "A low profile? Sounds like he was anything but low profile."

"Oh, it's complicated," she said. "And anyway, I'm starving."

We sat down to a simple dinner of barbequed chicken breasts and salad. I poked at the chicken but ate more than my share of salad.

Sunny looked at my plate. "Are you a vegetarian? I forgot to ask."

"No, I've been known to knock back many a harmless creature," I said. "But tonight I'm more tired than hungry, I guess. If you don't mind I'm going to head off to the *ohana* as soon as we've cleaned up the kitchen."

"Don't worry about it. My housekeeper comes tomorrow. I'll just throw the dishes in the dishwasher and leave the rest for her."

I went off to the guest house thinking how different my life would be if I could just pay someone else to clean up my messes.

***

On Monday, Sunny pulled up in front of the *ohana* in the Range Rover. "I'm going to drive since Timo's got things to do and who knows how long this court thing will take," she said.

We pulled in at the courthouse and Valentine was standing outside with a grim look on her face. I smiled as we approached but it wasn't returned.

"I don't want to go into it now," Valentine said when we'd gotten within earshot. "But the preliminary autopsy report on Peggy Chesterton has been released and it doesn't look good."

"They did an autopsy on a Sunday?" I said.

"Yes, Peggy's death is all over the news. After all, her father was the former mayor. I'm sure they called the ME right away and told him to get right on it."

"Well, don't leave us hanging," I said. "What didn't look good?"

"It seems she was extremely intoxicated at the time of the accident. But the tox screen was inconsistent with regular alcohol intoxication."

"So what made her drunk?"

"That's the million-dollar question. The ME is considering a more sophisticated test, but he says it might not be worth the trouble since the markers degrade with time and refrigeration."

Sunny shook her head. "Poor Peggy. Makes you wonder what happened. You know, come to think of it she didn't look at all good. I wonder if she might've been abusing pharmaceuticals or even street drugs."

"It's hard to imagine, but you never can tell," said Valentine. "Well, let's get inside. Judges don't suffer late-comers gladly."

We went up to the second floor. The courtroom was smaller than the one I'd been in on Maui, but then Kaua'i has half the number of residents of Maui. The judge was conferring with a court clerk when we slipped in and took our seats.

I'm not sure what I expected, but our courtroom appearance took only minutes. Valentine was approved as the executor of the estate and Sunny and I were noted as being the named beneficiaries in the will. It was all very matter-of-fact.

The judge ordered the notification period to begin. Documents were signed and stamped, fees were paid, and we were back outside in less than half an hour.

"That was easy," I said.

"Well," said Valentine. "What we accomplished today was simply to open probate. The process itself takes months, sometimes years. And if there's mediation involved—that is, if someone else comes forward to contest the will—then it can drag on and on."

"Oh, great," I said.

"But don't worry about it," said Valentine. "That's my job. Your job is to get the documents the judge requested. Sunny, I'll need originals of Phil's life insurance policies, deeds to the homes, and investment statements. Pali, all I need from you is your birth certificate."

I nodded. "I've got it at home."

"Go ahead and fax me a copy. Before the final settlement I'll need the original, but I have a hunch that will be months from now."

"So, we're done?" I said.

"I can't see any reason for you to stick around," said Valentine. "I can take you to the airport right now if you want."

Sunny and I hugged goodbye.

"Can I ask you a favor?" I said as Valentine and I walked through the parking lot. "Do you have time to drop me by the *The Garden Island* newspaper office? I need to check on something."

"Sure. I don't have appointments until after lunch. What do you need?"

"I'm hoping it will only take a minute. I want to see if there were any news stories about my mother's death back in 1981."

Valentine drove me to the office on Kuhio Highway and I went inside. She stayed in the car returning phone calls.

"*Aloha*, can I help you?" said a young local guy at the counter. "You want to set up a subscription?"

"No, I'm here to see if you can find something for me in your archives."

"We post our archives online, you know."

"Yes, and I checked it. But this is about a killing that happened in 1981."

He squinted up his face as if realizing I was going to be a tough customer. "I don't know what we'll have from back that far. We had a fire in the building in the middle eighties. Lost a lot of microfiche. Back then, we put all our archives on microfiche."

"Would you mind looking anyway?"

"Sure. Give me the date. I'll look it up and let you know if we have anything."

"Can I give you a month and year?"

He really squinted at that one. "That will take a while to go through. How about this? Do you have key words or maybe a name? We've put the big stories from the archives in a computer database. If I can find the exact date it will speed things up."

I gave him my mom's name, Marta Warner. I figured if they couldn't find it by her name then the microfiche had probably been lost in the fire.

He typed in the name.

"Ah. Seems we have a hit for Marta Warner on April 17, 1981," he said. "Would you like a copy? We charge a dollar a page for microfiche images. But I have to warn you; sometimes they're kind of blurry."

"That's okay. How many pages is it?"

"Um, looks like just one."

"Yes, please print it out for me."

He left, and a few minutes later he came back with the print-out. I took a dollar out of my purse.

"Nah. No charge. I looked at the story. Was she *ohana*?"

"Yeah. My mom."

"Sorry." He gave me a sympathetic nod and we held eye contact just a tad longer than was comfortable. "We publish good news too, you know? So if you ever want to sign up for home delivery…"

"*Mahalo*, but I live on Maui now."

I folded the print-out and went out to Valentine's car. She was still on the phone but she signed off a few seconds after I shut the door.

"Did you get what you needed?" she said.

"Yes, *mahalo*. I appreciate you waiting."

We drove for a minute and I said, "I was surprised to learn how long it's going to take to get the will through probate."

"Is it going to cause a hardship?" she said.

"No, but my car's sort of on its last legs."

"Oh. Well, sorry, but that's how probate works in Hawaii. I tried to talk your dad into a trust but he wouldn't consider it. I guess he had 'trust issues'." She turned and smiled as if she'd said something funny.

We got to the airport and she offered to park and come in to make sure I got a flight but I told her to go ahead and leave. "I'll get the next flight to Honolulu. From there, flights leave for Kahului every half-hour or so."

While I waited for them to call my flight to HNL I read the old newspaper account of my mother's death. Three times.

I learned nothing new. The only person named in the article was my mom. The story referred to the two men involved as simply 'North Shore residents.' The way it sounded, my mother had simply been in the wrong place at the wrong time and had taken a blow to the head. No mention of the police chief's son, not that that was surprising.

When I got on the plane, I buckled up and leaned back in my seat. I'd been gone less than three days but a lot had happened and some things didn't add up. Why had Joanie called my mom's death a murder if everyone else considered it an accident? And why had formerly clean and sober Peggy suddenly decided to fall off the wagon and drive into a tree? And why hadn't Phil come forward to get me when he heard my mother had died?

I was eager to get home. My brain worked better in familiar surroundings.

21

Steve picked me up at the airport. I slid into his spotless black Jetta and felt a little zing of envy. If things went as Valentine predicted, it would be months, maybe even a year or more, before I could get a new car. It was the one thing I wanted that money could buy.

"How are things at home?" I said.

The scowl on his face tipped me off. "Well, I guess if one enjoyed living in a hippie day care center they'd say 'great.' I, on the other hand, am finding the environment a bit challenging."

"What do you mean? One kid doesn't constitute a day care center."

"True, if there was only one. Farrah's up to three now," he said.

"Three? What's going on?"

"I should probably let her tell you herself. She asked me to stay out of it."

"Tell me, Steve. I have a hunch I may need to practice an eviction speech."

"Okay, so here's the situation so far: a woman dropped Moke off at the store. Then, on Saturday, Farrah did some of her *juju* nonsense and located his mother. That afternoon the mother showed up and she's got two other kids, twin girls. I'm not good with kid's ages, but I'd say they're around four or five. The mom looks barely eighteen, so I assume she was making babies when she should've been studying for a middle school algebra test. Anyway, she's got food stamps, but other than that, she's pretty much living on the street."

"Farrah's taken in all of this woman's kids?"

"Not exactly. She's agreed to raise Moke as her *hanai* kid, but she's watching the other two while their mother's out supposedly looking for a job. So, in the space of one weekend, my life has gone from perfecting the topping on my crème brulee to mastering the art of transforming powdered baby formula into liquid without lumps. And it's that soy stuff so it's always got lumps. And, it stinks to high heaven."

"*Three* kids?" I couldn't get past the number.

"Yep. And from the looks of things, the teenage mom's not going to score a job anytime soon."

"Are they all sleeping at the house?"

"Yep. On Saturday night it was just the kids. But then Farrah started babbling about 'it takes a village' and how she couldn't allow her 'sister/mom' to sleep outdoors anymore so last night we had the entire unwashed tribe." He shuddered. "I love Farrah, but I'm afraid if this is the way it's gonna be, then I'm going to start looking for new digs."

"Okay, don't get ahead of yourself. This is my house and I'm home now. I'll have a talk with her."

We got to the house and sure enough, the first thing I heard as I went in was the screech of little kids. I pushed through the swinging door from the kitchen and saw my living room in an utter uproar. There were blankets draped from the sofa to the coffee table and toys scattered everywhere.

I turned to Steve. "I thought you said these kids were homeless. How come they have so much stuff?"

"Farrah took them to Costco yesterday," he said.

"What's with the blankets?"

"When I left to pick you up there was talk about building a fort."

Farrah came down the stairs holding Moke. She was humming and softly patting his back. If I hadn't been so overwhelmed by the coup that had taken place I might've found the scene heartwarming.

"What's going on here?" I said.

"Pali, *ho'okipa*! Welcome home. Isn't it cute? The girls are playing house." We all turned and looked as two identical faces popped out from a gap in the blankets.

I took Farrah's elbow and guided her toward the kitchen. "Farrah, this is not okay. I can't have three kids in my house. This isn't how Steve and I want to live."

There was a loud knock at the front door.

"That must be Hatch," said Farrah. "He's so sweet. He heard you were coming home and offered to let us stay down at his place."

I went to the door.

"Hey Pali," he said. He slid by me saying, "Is Farrah in the kitchen?"

I nodded. He disappeared behind the swinging door and I heard laughing.

"Are you our other mommy?" said a tiny voice.

I looked down at a doll-like face peering up at me. She had jet-black hair with thick bangs and a smooth bob that fell to chin length. Her haircut was so precise it looked unnatural on a little kid.

"Uh, no, I guess you would call me your 'auntie'," I said. "Auntie Pali." It felt strange to introduce myself that way. I'd gone from having aunties to being one and it made me feel positively ancient.

"My name's Echo and my sister's name is Rain," she said. At the mention of her name, little Rain pulled aside the blanket to show her face. The two girls were so alike I felt like I'd lapsed into double-vision.

"Is this your house?" said Echo. "Mama says a rich lady owns this house."

I smiled. "Well, the bank owns this house. But I pay the bank to live here."

"Can we live here too? We'll tell Mama to pay the bank. We don't like to sleep outside. It's cold."

"And scary," said Rain.

Hatch and Farrah came out of the kitchen. Now Hatch was holding the baby. He was smacking the kid's back with such force I thought it must hurt. But then Moke let out a resounding burp and everyone laughed.

"Time to pack up, *keiki*," said Hatch. "We're moving down to the ranch."

"Can I have a minute with you?" I said.

"Sorry, but I've kind of got my hands full here," he said. "And I'm on shift tomorrow. How about I give you a call later?"

Hatch helped Farrah pack up the baby stuff in my bedroom and within ten minutes the house was deadly quiet.

I stood at the window. "What just happened?" I said to Steve as I watched Hatch's truck disappear down the street.

"Looks to me like you got dumped for some younger women."

***

Steve had to deliver some photo proofs to a client in Lahaina so I took the opportunity to go down to Palace of Pain to clear my head. I had no weddings on my calendar until late July but even if I had, I was in no shape to deal with people.

The sun was beginning to set as I headed down Baldwin Avenue. Chances were Sifu Doug would have already locked up and gone home but every black belt at PoP had been given a key so we could work out whenever we wanted.

I pulled in the alley and was surprised to see only one parking spot left. Ah, it was the first Monday of the month. Sifu Doug always scheduled promotion ceremonies on the first Monday. I considered driving through the alley and out the other side but as I passed the open door, Doug waved at me. He had a big smile on his face.

Busted. I pulled in and parked.

"Pali, *mahalo nui loa* for showing up," he said. He gripped my hand and started in on one of his fancy handshake routines. I found all the fist-bumping and elaborate hand-jiving silly but it was part of the male culture I'd fought hard to join, so I went with it.

"How many are getting promoted tonight?" I said.

"Just six. Four yellow belts and a couple green. Shouldn't take too long. And the moms brought some *ono*-looking casseroles."

"Sounds great."

We went inside and Sifu Doug started the ceremony. It'd been a long time since I'd attended a promotion and I'd forgotten how solemn and emotional the ritual could be. Four little kids were getting their yellow belt, the first belt in the sequence. There was a lot of bowing and smiling, with parents taking photo after photo. I watched, and for the first time in a long time, I wondered if I was missing out on something by not having kids.

When the ceremony was over Sifu Doug announced it was time to eat. He laid down the law that the kids should show respect by allowing their parents and elders to go through the line first. This was new to most of the kids. In Hawaii, the usual order of things is kids always get first dibs. But when Sifu Doug barked an order in his ex-Army Ranger voice, nobody argued.

I scooped up a bit of salad and Spam casserole and sat on the floor with my back to the wall. After Doug had made sure everyone had food and he'd posed for photos with each of the graduates, he came and sat by me.

"How you doin'?" he said. "I heard you were over on Kaua'i. And it looks like Farrah found the baby's mother."

In a small town like Pa'ia I would've been surprised if he hadn't heard.

"Yep. According to Farrah, she did her thing with the Ouija board and voila! she managed to track down the mother. I haven't met her yet. Steve says she's looking for a job."

"She cuts hair, right? I heard she's some kind of hair stylist or something."

I thought about the twins' perfectly cut hair and put two and two together. "I guess that's right."

"You know, Lani's got a friend who works down at the beauty shop at the Westin. I could ask her if they've got room for another girl." Sifu Doug wasn't much older than I but he refused to budge from talking like an old-timer. To him, all women were 'girls' and anyone involved in manual labor was a 'boy.' Luckily, he was such a nice guy no one took offense.

"*Mahalo*. But that's a pretty swanky salon for a homeless woman," I said. "You think they'd consider her?"

"All the more reason." Doug's world view matched his speech. He stuck to the ancient Polynesian philosophy of giving to each according to their needs. The most down-and-out should be helped first. To me, it ran counter to martial arts training where only the strong survive, but somehow he managed to play it from both sides.

He went on. "I hope you're okay that I told James not to call you. After Farrah and the mom got together over the weekend I figured it was cool. No sense borrowing trouble."

I put my plate down on the floor and drew my legs up under me. "I suppose. But I'm still worried the mother might change her mind."

"I doubt it," he said. "The whole town knows Moke is Farrah's now."

Doug got up and thanked everyone for coming to the promotion. Parents gathered up kids, casserole dishes and promotion certificates and ushered their broods outside. Inside, I started picking up trash and wiping sticky spilled punch off the training mats.

"Hey, thanks again for coming down," said Doug as he folded down the legs on the eight-foot serving tables and dragged them into the storage room.

"I know you want to get home to Lani and the kids, but can I talk to you for just a minute?"

"Sure. Fire away."

I filled him in on Peggy's death and how the Kaua'i cops had made me feel somehow responsible. "The autopsy showed she was heavily intoxicated, but they say it's 'inconsistent' with normal blood alcohol readings. When she showed up where I was staying she was drunk, but not *that* drunk."

"Lots of stuff can make you act drunk," said Doug. "I took a bioterrorism class in Army Ranger training. Maybe somebody poisoned her."

"Poisoned? But wouldn't a tox screen pick that up?"

"Hard to say. If it's something unusual, routine tox screens might not find it. I know they have to do special tests to check for things like anthrax and sarin."

I thanked him and went out to my car. I hadn't had a chance to get in a work out, but I felt more relaxed than I had in days.

22

I went in to my shop on Tuesday if for no other reason than to get out of the house and back to my normal routine. The phone on my desk wasn't blinking, which meant I had no messages. At about ten-thirty I wandered over to the Gadda da Vida but Farrah wasn't at the counter. Instead there was a young woman with silky black hair that nearly reached her waist.

"Hi," I said. "I'm Pali Moon. I own the wedding planning business next door."

"Oh, cool. I'm Shadow. Farrah told me about you. My kids and me stayed at your place this weekend." She nodded and kept nodding like one of those bobble-head dolls on a car dashboard. "Yeah, like thanks for letting us hang out there."

"You're welcome," I said. I felt guilty. I wondered how Farrah had framed my coming home and them having to find a new place to stay.

"So, now you're all staying at Hatch Deckers' place?"

"Yeah. He is so cool. A really sweet guy. And he just *loves* my kids."

I joined in the nodding but stopped after a couple of bobs to avoid the two of us looking like mating albatrosses.

"What did you come in for?" she said. She waved toward the aisles of groceries. "I'm trying to learn where everything is. A lady wanted lemon juice in a bottle and so far that's the only thing I still can't find. "

"It's on aisle six, top shelf," I said. "For some reason Farrah shelves it with the vinegar instead of the fruit juice."

"That makes total sense. *Mahalo.*"

"Are you planning to be working here for long?" I said. As soon as I'd said it I realized it sounded kind of snarky. Like I wanted to kick her out of there too. "I mean, Farrah mentioned you've been looking for a job."

"Nah, I'm just helping out. Farrah offered to watch the kids today. I can't believe how cool she is. I mean, I was one inch from driving off a cliff after I had Moke. I got a great vibe off Farrah when I came in here a few days after he got born. You know, even though I was using food stamps and WIC vouchers and stuff she still treated me with respect. And she didn't sic the cops on me or nothing after I left Moke here. And then when she did her psychic thing and figured out it was me! I was totally blown away. She's totally righteous, you know?"

"That she is."

A group of four customers came in and I used the opportunity to slip out the back. I was headed for my shop when my cell phone chimed.

"Hello?"

"Hello Pali, it's Valentine Fabares. I haven't received your birth certificate yet. Did you fax it?"

I'd completely forgotten. "Oh sorry. I'll send it today. It's been crazy since I've been back. Not a minute's rest."

"I'm sure. Well I promised the court I'd submit everything this week so fax it over here as soon as possible, okay?"

"Will do."

I hung up and kept walking up the alley. My birth certificate was in a safety deposit box at the bank. I didn't keep it there because I was worried about losing it or having it stolen. It was there because the bank offered me a free deposit box when I opened my business account and I wanted to take advantage of every perk.

A sour-faced bank clerk took me into the vault and pulled out a skinny metal drawer from the bank of boxes. Then she ceremoniously placed it on a table in the middle of the room. In a hushed voice she said, "Take as long as you need. When you're finished, let me know and I'll lock it back up." Her demeanor was so glum I was sure if her bank job didn't work out she could easily snag a gig at the funeral home behind the hardware store.

I thanked her and rifled through the small stack of items in the box. There was my passport, the deed to my house, and my birth certificate. I flipped open the passport and stared at the photo. It looked like someone had goosed me a second before they'd snapped the picture. Even though my passport had been issued in my real name, they'd allowed me to also add 'Pali Moon' since I had so much ID showing that name.

I laid the passport back in the box and took out my birth certificate. It had been folded into a business envelope with a post office box as the return address. When had I gotten it? I couldn't remember. I stuck the envelope in my purse and alerted the bank clerk I was done.

"That was fast," she said.

How long did she expect me to take? Did people go into the vault and try on every piece of their *tutu's* jewelry or count out bags of gold coins like a crazy miser?

We used our keys to lock the drawer in place and I thanked her.

"No, thank *you* for doing business with us here at Royal Hawaiian Bank and Trust." Forget the funeral job. It sounded like she was bucking for promotion. There were cameras everywhere so she must've hoped some bigwig was watching.

I took the birth certificate to my shop and plugged in my fax machine. I rarely used the thing but when I needed to send an important document I preferred it to a scanner. Who knows where a scanned file might end up on the Internet?

When the fax had gone through, I took the certificate out of the machine and looked at it. On the line for father they'd typed the name, Coyote P. Moon. How weird that for my entire life I'd known that name but didn't have a single clue about the person behind it. In my teen years I'd imagined my father to be someone famous. Maybe a rocker like Gene Simmons from Kiss or a world-class athlete who'd had to leave when he got word he'd been selected for the 1976 Summer Olympics team.

Later, I found out about the legions of 1970's counter-culture kids who'd scraped together enough money to fly to Hawaii and then had just stuck around. They surfed and smoked weed and mooched off the government for as long as possible before either maturity or family pressure called them back to the mainland.

Apparently my father had fallen into the latter category.

I folded the birth certificate and put it back in the envelope. I sat at my desk, staring out the front window and pondering everything that had happened in the past week. I'd learned my precious mother had died trying to save my brother's dad from the police chief's pot-head son. And my dad had returned to Hawaii and became a wealthy businessman who chose to never reveal himself to me until he died. And then he'd willed me millions of dollars while totally excluding his other children. His first wife had just died in a drinking and driving wreck and, for some reason, the cops think I had something to do with it. Then, after all that, I come home to my best friend becoming a new mother and my "Rookie of the Year" boyfriend playing the gracious host to two women and three kids.

Last week had been over-the-moon bizarre. This week couldn't help but be better.

***

About half an hour after I'd faxed Valentine the birth certificate I got a call. "Hello Pali, it's Valentine again. Say, I'm afraid I'm going to have to ask another favor."

"Okay."

"I appreciate you faxing your birth record, but the court will require an attested birth certificate."

"So the fax won't do? Do you want me to mail it to you?" I said.

"No, that won't help. I need a certified copy of the original long form birth certificate. The document you faxed to me isn't a legal document. It's just a birth record. It doesn't contain any signatures."

"But that's all I have. When I applied for my passport they accepted it."

"Yes, well the federal government has latitude with these things. The courts view it differently."

"What can I do?"

"You should be able to get a copy of your birth certificate from the state records office in Honolulu. You can order one by mail but it'll take too long. I need a copy by Friday. The records office will want ID and a document stating this is an urgent request. I'll fax you a letter to take with you."

"So this means another plane ride?" I said.

"Didn't your dad mention you were an air marshal at one time?"

"Point taken. It's just that I'm not getting any work done here. I need to—"

"Pali, after you get me that birth certificate, this probate can get underway. And once probate's been settled, your job will be the least of your concerns." She said it with a smile in her voice but it made me cringe.

"You said it could take months or even a year. I've still got to make my house payment."

"Of course. But right now, the most important thing is to get that birth certificate to me ASAP."

"I'll go tomorrow," I said.

"Tomorrow's a holiday. Try to get the earliest flight out on Thursday," said Valentine.

"Oh wow, I forgot. Tomorrow's the Fourth of July."

"Yes, no mail, no banks, and no government offices." There was a beat of dead air and then she went on in a cheery voice, "Have you made plans for the holiday?"

"Not yet. But I'm still playing catch-up from being gone. I'll probably just hang around the house."

"Well, whatever you do, have a relaxing day. And please give me a call when you get that certificate."

We said our good-byes. I looked up the website for Hawaii birth records and found I'd have to go to the Department of Health, Vital Records Division on Punchbowl Street in downtown Honolulu. I understood why Valentine had advised me to get an early flight. The office was only open from 7:45 in the morning to 2:30 in the afternoon.

I'd hoped to hear from Hatch but it was already three o'clock and so far, nothing. I sat at my desk willing the phone to ring until I'd had enough. I locked up and went down to Palace of Pain. I went full-tilt, no holds barred. It worked. I'd learned long ago that one way to avoid fretting was to start sweating.

23

After spending the Fourth of July washing my car, doing laundry, and generally just moping around the house, Steve allowed me to tag along with him to the Independence Night Blowout at the Ball and Chain. The B & C was his gay bar of choice in Kihei; a town known more for family-friendly vacation rentals than Calvin Klein underwear models. The proprietor had decked the place out in red, white and blue bunting and balloons and he'd strewn glittery confetti stars over every possible horizontal space.

When we walked in someone yelled Steve's name from a table in the corner. We both turned. It was Levi. He waved us over to join him.

"You chat him up," Steve whispered in my ear. "I'll go grab us some drinks. Meet me at my usual spot."

Levi asked about Farrah and I filled him in as best I could about Farrah tracking down the baby's birth mother and them coming to an agreement about Farrah raising the boy as her *hanai* son.

"I don't get it," he said. "You can do that? I mean, don't you have to go to court or something?"

"Nah, the Hawaiians have been taking care of family stuff like this for more than a century. It's like they say, *We don't need no stinkin' badges*."

"Well, that's good I guess. Say, what's with Steve? He's really been avoiding me lately. Did I do something wrong?"

If he had, Steve hadn't let me in on it. I shrugged. "Sometimes he's like that. When was the last time you bought him a drink?"

Levi bolted from the table and headed toward the bar.

Steve came over with a glass of chardonnay for me and a club soda for himself. "What was that about?" he said. "Levi practically vaulted over the bar to pay for this round."

"He thinks you're shutting him out," I said. "I asked him if he'd shown appropriate patronage to his don."

"Oh great. I guess you're still hung up on the mafia thing."

"Hey, if the shoe fits. So are you?"

"Are I what?"

"Are you shutting him out?"

"No," he said. "Not intentionally."

"Trouble in paradise?"

"I guess it's something like that. You'll notice I'm here with you tonight and Steven's nowhere in sight."

"So, which is it? Has Steven got a thing for Levi or the other way around?" I said.

Steve shook his head. "Don't even ask."

"Sheesh, look at us," I said. "I've got Hatch troubles and you're pining over Steven. Our lives are like a pathetic reality show."

"Yeah," he said. "Except neither of us is getting rich or famous in the process."

I sucked down the rest of my chard and then put my hand on his. "Can you keep a secret?"

The rest of the night passed in a hazy blur of bad chardonnay, dancing to the soundtrack from 'Glee,' and trips to a stifling 'ladies' room where half of the 'ladies' were guys in drag hogging the mirror.

***

I woke up early Thursday morning with a headache and a throbbing pinky-toe.

"Coffee?" said Steve as I stumbled into the kitchen.

"Can you set up an I-V? I think my throat's on strike."

"You were pretty funny last night. I mean, it's kind of fun to be the designated driver. If I were diabolical I could've gotten enough photos to blackmail you out of a year's rent."

"Did Steven ever make an appearance?" I said. It was unkind of me to bring up Steve's bruised love life, but I didn't want to suffer alone. I poured myself some coffee and dumped in cream and sugar.

"Yeah, actually he did. In fact, he's still asleep upstairs."

So much for misery looking for a little company.

"You guys made up?"

"Yeah. I was just being touchy, I guess. He said he'd seen me introducing Levi around and thought he should do his bit."

"And what was his 'bit'?"

"He danced with him most of last Saturday night."

"Some 'bit'."

"Yeah, but it's okay. I've gotten over myself."

I put two more spoonful's of sugar in my coffee.

"Didn't you already put in sugar?" Steve said.

"I'm not feeling very sweet this morning. I guess it's time for me to consider getting over myself too. I haven't heard a peep from either Hatch or Farrah since Monday. And I've got to leave again this morning."

"Didn't you see your message? Hatch left a voicemail on Tuesday. I wrote it down." He got up and rifled around by the phone until he came up with a scrap of paper. In his precise handwriting it said, *Picnic Honokowai Beach Pk. 7/4 at 3pm, Call Hatch.*

"Why didn't you tell me about this?"

"Hey, I wrote it down. You need to check for messages. I always put them right here by the phone." Steve sounded irked but it was probably to cover up his guilt for forgetting to tell me about it.

"I'll call him later this afternoon." I checked the wall clock. "First, I need to make a quick trip to Honolulu to pick up my birth certificate."

"For court?"

"Yeah. Valentine said the thing I've been using for a birth certificate isn't official. I've got to go to the state records office and get a certified copy."

Now that Steve knew about my possible inheritance he was eager to help me get it. He offered to drive me to the airport.

"And I don't mind parking and walking you up to security."

"Hey, hold off on the major sucking up," I said. "I haven't seen a penny yet and according to the lawyer, these things take months. Sometimes years."

He was undeterred. "Still, you're an heiress-in-waiting. That's good enough for me."

When we pulled up to the white zone it seemed like even the airport was nursing a hangover. In the open-air lobby there was hardly anyone in the check-in lines. The sky caps were leaning against the posts gabbing with each other.

"Just drop me off," I said. "I'll make the next flight, no problem."

I was waiting at the gate for the eight-fifteen flight to be called when my cell phone rang. Good. It was probably Hatch calling to say he'd missed me at the picnic. I prepared myself to act indignant that Steve hadn't given me the message.

"*Aloha*," I sang into the phone.

It was Valentine. "So glad I caught you. I called and called last night but you never picked up."

Since when is it a serious breach of conduct to be out of touch for a few hours? But maybe in Valentine's world—where her clients are using their one phone call from jail—it is.

She went on. "Anyway, where are you now?"

"I'm in the Kahului airport. I'm on the next flight to Honolulu."

"Good. We need that birth certificate. Will you be bringing it over to Kaua'i?"

"I was hoping I could just fax it."

"Yes, well I thought that would work, but this morning I learned the judge is insisting on originals. He's taking a two-week vacation starting tomorrow so if we don't get this locked up before then, it will be put aside until he returns. And after he returns he'll be swamped with backlog. Do you see where this is going?"

"Yes."

"Can you indulge me by catching a flight as soon as you get the certificate?"

"Can't I just send it with a courier?"

"I don't want to go into all the times I've had couriers drop the ball," Valentine said.

Another trip to Kaua'i was right up there with a root canal or jury duty, but I had no excuse. I had no wedding business pending and my personal life had flat-lined. I told Valentine I'd come. I got in line for my Honolulu flight and shut down my phone. It looked like I wouldn't be getting together with Hatch for at least another day.

24

I arrived in Honolulu in the middle of rush hour. But then, there are only a couple of hours in the dead of night when it isn't rush hour in Honolulu. I snagged a cab and gave him the address for the Vital Records Office.

"It's near the corner of Beretania and Punchbowl," I added. "Right downtown." I didn't want him to think I was a mainlander who'd enjoy taking the scenic route and paying twice as much.

"You on jury duty?"

"No."

"You getting divorced?"

"No."

"Then why you going to court?"

"I'm not going to the courthouse. I'm going to the Department of Health."

"You sick?"

"Look, it's early. I've had nowhere near my normal consumption of coffee and the traffic's horrible," I said. "Would you mind just getting me where I need to go?"

"Hey, I jus' trying to be friendly. At a drivers' meeting las' week they say riders tip better if you're friendly. Ask how their doing, what's up with their family, that sorta t'ing."

"I promise I'll tip better if you just get me there fast. No talking."

That was the wrong thing to say. The guy veered off at the next exit and roared through industrial back alleys like a cop in hot pursuit. He kept flicking his eyes up to check the rear view mirror. I wanted to tell him to knock off the stunt driving, but I'd already said enough.

We screeched to a halt in front of the Department of Health. He turned around in his seat and said, "That fast enough for ya?"

I pulled out two twenty's for a thirty-dollar fare and told him to keep the change.

"*Mahalo*. You want I should wait for you?"

I sent him on his way and went inside. Hawaiian state government prides itself on its world-class bureaucracy. What takes two government workers on the mainland requires at least six people in Hawaii. I steeled myself for the gauntlet ahead.

The process to get my birth certificate turned out to be less taxing then I'd expected. I had to wait half-an-hour for them to locate the record and apply the certification seal, but I had it in hand within an hour. I was about to head outside when it occurred to me that I'd never seen a copy of my mother's death certificate. Even when I went through Auntie Mana's 'special papers' after she'd passed, I never came across anything regarding my mother's death.

I went to the end of the line. When I got to the counter, I was directed to a different window than before. I explained to the ample-sized local woman working the window that I'd like to get a copy of my mother's death certificate.

"You lose the first one?" she said in a sympathetic whisper.

I didn't know what the right answer should be. Had I lost the one I'd been given? If so, it shouldn't be a problem to replace it. On the other hand, what kind of daughter thinks so little of her *ohana* that she misplaces important family documents?

So, instead of answering, I puckered up my face as if the whole thing was distressing beyond words.

"No worries," said the clerk. "Just fill in this form and come back. No need you do the line again."

I took the form to a table and filled it out using the information my mother had provided on my birth certificate. Then I went back to the window. The clerk typed on her computer and looked up.

"Okay, here it is," she said. "Do you need just your mother's death certificate or do you want her marriage certificate, too?"

"Uh, both if possible. *Mahalo.*" Had my mother and father actually gotten married? I was having a hard time keeping up with the onslaught of new family information.

"I'm afraid it's gonna take a few days to get you the certified copies. Is this is an urgent request?"

I'd used the letter from Valentine to get my birth certificate right away, but I didn't have anything like that for my mother's documents.

"No. It's important, but not urgent."

"We'll send it to you. Shouldn't take more than a couple days."

"That will be fine, *mahalo*." I paid the fees and left the window. I thought about taking the bus to the airport but it was getting late and Valentine would be getting anxious. I was already anxious. My parents had actually married? Why hadn't Auntie Mana told me that?

I called for a cab and hoped it wouldn't be the same driver. A decrepit yellow taxi with shot shocks pulled up to the building and a woman driver popped out and waved me over. I got in and we made it to the airport with little fanfare. I gave her forty bucks even though the meter showed only twenty-eight. I believe in equal pay for equal work, and besides, she hadn't made my adrenaline spike.

I bought a ticket for the ten-thirty flight to Lihue but then noticed there was an earlier flight leaving in seven minutes. I took off running. The gate agent shot me major *stink eye* as I came ripping up to the podium. They'd already closed the jet-way door.

"Sorry. I got detained at security," I said, handing over my crumpled boarding pass.

She looked at me with eyes that said, *Liar, liar, pants on fire*.

"Really," I huffed. "I didn't have any luggage and I must've looked shifty or something 'cuz I got treated to the full body pat-down." I sucked in a deep breath. "Heaven knows I understand the need for security. I was a federal air marshal for a while. So don't worry, I'm one of the good guys." I shot her what I hoped passed for a winsome smile.

She glared as if this was a common ploy of would-be hijackers. "This boarding pass is for our next flight, not this one."

"I know, but I need to get to Lihue as fast as possible," I said. "I have an important meeting with a Hanalei lawyer."

She softened a little, realizing only a local would be meeting with a small town lawyer.

"Take the first seat available," she said in a steely voice. She punched in the code to the jet-way door. "You've already delayed this departure four minutes."

***

As we were landing I pulled out my cellphone but I waited until the flight attendant gave us the go-ahead before calling Valentine.

"You're here?" she said. "Do you have the birth certificate?"

"Yes, all signed, sealed and as soon as this plane makes it to the gate, delivered."

"I'm afraid I won't be able to pick you up. I'm already at the courthouse and if I leave I'll lose my place in line. Would you mind taking a cab?"

"Sure, no problem." Airplane tickets and taxi fares had already made a big dent in my wallet, but the Lihue courthouse was only a few minutes from the airport. As I exited the terminal my cell went off again.

"Pali? It's Sunny. I just got to the courthouse and Valentine tells me you need a ride. I'll send Timo."

The white Range Rover came into view within minutes. He hustled around and opened the back door but I nodded toward the front passenger seat.

"Have it your way," he said. His voice had a gruff edge, but he was smiling. "Mrs. Wilkerson tells me you're Phil's daughter. You jus' like him, man."

We arrived at the courthouse and Timo dropped me at the door. I hustled inside. Sunny was standing in the lobby.

"Valentine's over in the records office. She asked me to wait out here for you."

"Did you know Phil actually had *seven* wives?" I said.

"What? Did someone call from the notification Valentine put in the newspaper? It's probably just some gold digger."

"No, it wasn't from the paper," I said. "It appears my *mom* was married to Phil."

"And why would you think that?"

"Because I was just at the Vital Records Office in Honolulu and my mom's got a marriage certificate on file."

"Huh. Well, that's a shocker." She looked more pensive than shocked. "C'mon. We better get your birth certificate to Valentine."

25

After I'd located Valentine in the county clerk's office and handed over my birth certificate, Sunny offered to buy me coffee. It was past noon, and I'd only had one quick cup with Steve more than six hours earlier.

"You didn't know my father and mother had been married?" I said.

"I don't remember Phil mentioning it. He probably felt so bad about what happened to her he didn't want to dwell on it. I always thought Peggy was his first wife. Remember, that's what he said in his will."

"Speaking of Peggy," I lowered my voice to a whisper. "Have you heard anything more?"

"Not a thing."

Valentine showed up a few minutes later. "It's all set," she said. "The judge is taking a two-week vacation, but we've got the clock ticking on the probate. There's not much more we can do until the notification period is over." She looked down at her watch. "I'm afraid I need to leave. I have an appointment in an hour up in Hanalei. Thanks for coming on such short notice, Pali. I hope you won't have to make any more trips over here for a while."

We shook hands and Valentine left.

"I guess I better get to the airport," I said. "It feels like I've spent more time in airports in the past couple of weeks than when I was an air marshal."

***

I landed in Maui and once again, Steve picked me up.

"How'd it go?" he said as I slid into the passenger seat.

"Well, other than feeling like I'm getting jet lag from so many interisland flights, I'd say it went pretty well. The probate's underway now."

"Great. So, did they give you any idea when you'll be rich?"

"Don't hold your breath. Oh, I did find out something interesting, though."

"Yeah?"

"Seems my parents were married after all."

"No kidding? How'd you find out?"

"I ordered my mother's wedding certificate at the Vital Records office."

"Wow," he said. "It's like pulling on a loose thread and, before you know it, you've unraveled the whole sweater. All it took was finding out who your dad was and now you've figured out your whole family story."

Steve had to go across the island to pick up a check and he asked if I wanted to go along. I declined, saying I had some things I needed to get done at my shop. I doubted if I'd actually get much work done, but I hadn't seen Farrah or Hatch for three days and I had fences to mend.

I asked him to drop me off at Farrah's store. She was busy with a customer so I waited. When the customer left, Farrah came over and gave me a warm hug. She still smelled like 'baby' but I would've been concerned if she hadn't.

"Are you still staying down at Hatch's?" I said.

"Yeah, but not for long. It's kinda tight with three *keiki*, two dogs and three humans." I wanted to point out that technically *keiki*, or kids, were also human, but I didn't since I was mending fences.

"Where are you moving to?"

"I guess I'll move back up here. Everyone's been totally cool with me taking in Moke, so it's no big deal. His birth mom and me are real tight. In fact, we're doing a baptism this weekend."

"In a church?" I said.

"No, I'm a minister, remember? Wherever I am it's a church." That sounded a little 'diva' to me, but again, I was mending fences so I kept my mouth shut.

"Where are you having it?"

"Down at Ho'okipa Beach. It'll be fun. And guess what?"

"Uh, I don't know."

"No, you gotta guess." I usually refuse to go along with Farrah's guessing games but in the spirit of making amends, I relented.

"Okay, my guess is you're going to baptize all the kids. Even Echo and Rain."

"Good guess, 'cuz you're right. But there's more."
Oh boy, more.

"Let's see. Okay, my second guess is you've timed it to happen on a full moon." I was simply making stuff up until I could reasonably put an end to the guessing.

"Wow. Right again! It's so far out you'd think of that. You must be channeling me or something. Okay, one more guess. We should go until you get one wrong."

"Are you doing the baptism at night, so you can see the moon?"

"Oh, bummer. You got it wrong. No, it'll be in the day time. It'd be hard to get pictures at night. Steve offered to be the photographer—for free."

Funny. Steve hadn't mentioned anything about the baptism when he picked me up.

"How many people are coming?" I said.

"About eighty."

"*Eighty*? That's bigger than my biggest beach wedding all year."

"Yeah, but don't worry. I'm not gonna ask you to help with it or anything. Because…" She paused and I heard a drumroll in my head. "Because I'm asking you to be Moke's *akua*-mother, his 'goddess'-mother!"

Judging from the 'ta-dah' in her voice I figured she expected me to squeal in delight.

"*Mahalo*, I'm so honored." I said. I clasped my hands to my chest to make up for the lack of a squeal. In my mind I was wondering what it meant to be someone's 'goddess-mother'. I'd never heard of such a thing, so I had no idea what I'd just signed on for.

"When should I show up?" I said.

"We're going to start around four in the afternoon. Afterwards, Hatch has offered to tap a keg and lay out some heavy *pu'pu's*. It'll be fun."

I love the word *pu'pu*. It's what locals call 'appetizers.' Since I deal with mainlanders who want appetizers at their wedding dinner, I'm used to jumping in with a clarification when a caterer mentions *pu'pus* and the bride grimaces in disgust.

"Sounds great. So eighty people, huh?"

"Yep. And you and Hatch have both agreed to be Moke's *akua*-parents. I'm so excited." She leaned in for another tight hug.

Hatch had agreed to be the *akua*-father? Great. I wasn't sure of what I'd gotten myself into, but regardless of the job description, I had less than a day to tidy up a big hole in my relationship fence.

***

Farrah told me Hatch had gone to work that morning, which meant he'd be off the next two days. I called his cell.

"Decker," he said. There was no way he didn't know it was me. He'd even programmed in a special ring tone just for me.

"Hi 'Decker'," I said. I regretted it immediately. I tried to come up with a good save but he jumped in first.

"Hi, yourself. So, how is Hawaii's newest heiress doing this fine afternoon?"

Busted. I didn't know what to say.

"Yeah," he went on. "Nice of you to clue me in on the high points of your life. What'd you think? That I wouldn't find out?"

"Who told you?" As if I didn't know.

"Who cares? What matters is it wasn't you."

"I'm sorry. I didn't mean to keep it from you, but it's not a done deal."

"What's going on, Pali? One minute I feel like we're making headway and the next I feel like I'm on the bottom of the pile."

"A lot has happened, Hatch. You've been busy and I've been gone—"

He cut me off. "Sorry. Hear that? We're getting called out. I promised to help a guy move tomorrow. So, I guess I'll see you on Saturday at the kids' baptism."

The only saving grace was I could hear the siren going off in the station. Seems he really did need to go.

***

On Friday I got up early and went down to the Palace of Pain. I hadn't slept well and I was sure it showed. When I pulled up, Sifu Doug was hosing down a mat in the alley.

"*Aloha*, Sifu," I said.

"*Aloha*, Pali. How you doin'? I hear Farrah's going to be moving back to her apartment. Seems the *hanai* thing is working out okay." He followed me inside.

"Yeah, it turned out good." I waited. Sifu Doug was a sixth degree black belt. He knew how to time his attack.

"You down here to practice? Sorry to say, but you look kinda gnarly."

"I feel gnarly. Not much sleep last night."

"You having man trouble again?"

I nodded. "That and a few other things."

"Tell you what. You buy me a Gatorade and you can tell me about it. I don't have classes 'til ten."

"How about I get in an hour of practice and then I'll buy you that Gatorade?"

"Deal."

I kicked and punched for nearly an hour but my heart wasn't in it. My body felt weakened by the weight of the last six days. I plugged quarters into the vending machine and joined Doug in his office.

I handed him an orange Gatorade. "What're you working on?"

"I like the green better," he said eying my bottle. I handed it over. I recognize an alpha move when I see one. "I'm doing a little bookkeeping," he said. Then he grinned. "Unlike some people, I gotta keep track of my money. I didn't have a rich daddy."

"So you heard."

"Of course I heard. Whaddaya think this is, Antarctica? You tell somebody somethin' juicy, it's gonna drip down."

"Well, I guess my father leaving me a bunch of money is big gossip around here, but that's not what's on my mind."

"Oh yeah? What's more important than thirty million bucks?"

"I'm not getting thirty million. It'll be around half that."

"Well, whether it's a couple million or a hundred million, it's still millions more than I'll ever see. So what's keeping you up nights?"

"I suppose it's useless to swear you to secrecy," I said.

"I'm better than most, but you know it's like holding your breath. As hard as you try, everyone cracks."

I told him how my relationship with Hatch had become strained to the breaking point. I'd missed his awards banquet; he'd had to take in Farrah and her kid when they were no longer welcome at my place; and now he'd learned about my inheritance through a third party rather than from me.

"I read in *The Maui News* Hatch made Rookie of the Year," said Doug. "That's a big deal. Why didn't you go with him?"

"I didn't mean to. I had a new dress and everything. But one of my father's ex-wives was on her way out of town and she called and asked me to meet her in Honolulu. She said she'd tell me about my mother being killed. And then I couldn't get a flight back here in time for the banquet."

"Whoa, whoa, whoa. What's that? Your say you mother was *killed*? Like murdered?"

"Yeah. It's an awful story." I filled him in on the details.

"The police chief's kid killed your mom?"

"Yep."

Doug seemed to consider the enormity of the accusation.

Then he said, "Wow. And it happened thirty years ago?"

"Yes, but there's no statute of limitations on murder."

"Yeah, I know. So, what are you gonna do about it?"

"Right now it's just hearsay," I said. "I don't have any evidence."

"Well, maybe when you come into all that dough you'll be able to hire somebody. You know, like a private eye or something." He paused, then went on. "And that brings up the next question. Why'd you keep Hatch in the dark about your dad leaving you the big bucks?"

"Because the lawyer says I won't see any of it for months, maybe a year or more. I didn't think it was appropriate to tell Hatch until it was a done deal."

"Appropriate? Really? Let me tell you something, Pali. If Lani kept me in the dark about something as big as that, I'd be totally steamed. Especially if she'd already blabbed to other people."

"I know. I should've told him. But I still haven't decided if I'm going to take any of it. I was worried he might try to change my mind."

"What're you talkin' about? Of course you're gonna take it. It's yours."

"I don't know. I've been noticing people with money. And you know what? They never seem to be decent people. My dad sure wasn't decent. Leaving my mom, who I now know was his *wife*, and then dumping me off on Auntie Mana."

He shot me a sardonic smile. "Tell you what. I'll do you a favor. You take the money. If it turns you all mean and nasty, I'll take it off your hands. No worries 'cuz everybody knows I'm already mean and nasty."

He walked me to the door. "*Mahalo* for the Gatorade. But don't expect me to buy the next round." He gave me a little punch in the shoulder.

I bowed in respect and went out to my car. I spent the rest of Friday down in Kahului shopping for baptism gifts. I still wasn't sure what it meant to be a 'goddess-mother.' But I was pretty sure gifts were part of the deal.

26

On Saturday morning Steve knocked on my bedroom door. "Hey sleepy-head," he said. "It's almost ten-thirty."

"Hang on a second," I got up and slipped on the kimono Hatch had bought me in Kaua'i and I felt a pang of sadness.

I opened the door. Steve was leaning against the doorframe. "You know we've got that baptism today," he said.

"Yeah, but it isn't until four."

"But we're taking formal pictures at two-thirty. And it takes about a half-hour to get down there, and we've got to find a place to park, and I've got to set up my gear, and—"

"Okay, okay. You go on ahead. I'll meet you down there at two-thirty."

He shot me his *tsk tsk* look. "There are about a hundred people coming and it's Saturday. No way you'll find a parking spot within a half-mile of Ho'okipia."

"I thought Farrah said she'd invited eighty people."

"She called last night. It's now up to nearly a hundred."

"Sheesh. Okay, give me half an hour."

I took a shower and even shaved my legs. Then I slipped on a clean pair of white capris, a bright aloha print shirt and a pair of white *rubba slippas* with little painted flowers. Since Steve was going to be taking pictures I took my time swiping on mascara and blushing my cheekbones. I glossed up my lips and checked my image in the mirror. Not bad. I grabbed my beach bag purse and went to get something to eat to tide me over.

I pushed through the kitchen door.

"Is that what you're wearing?" said Steve.

I looked down to see if I'd missed a big soy sauce stain on my pants or something. "Yeah. What's the problem?"

"Well, from what I've been told, you're supposed to be the 'goddess-mother'. But I don't see much 'goddess' goin' on with those crop pants and that tired old aloha shirt. Do you need me to explain the concept of professional photos?"

"Give me another minute."

I charged back into my room and dug through my top drawer for the pearl 'amulet' Farrah had given me for my birthday. I put it around my neck but after three tries I still couldn't get the clasp to work.

Steve stood in my bedroom doorway. "Oh, get over here." He fastened it and then put both hands on my shoulders and turned me around to face him. "Look, Pali. I've got something to say and I hope you take it in the spirit of love and friendship."

"Well, that's an ominous lead-in," I said.

"I know. But I want you to listen. Lately, you've been really caught up in this thing with your mom, and I totally understand. But you've already missed your boyfriend's big night and today is a huge day for your best friend. Do I need to say more?"

I looked down. "I've got it, and you're right."

"So, let's go down there and put on the happy face. And if you don't kiss and make up with Hatch, I'll be beyond disappointed in you. Although it pains me to point it out, you're not getting any younger and you're still very single."

"Okay, don't push it. I already said you're right."

We hardly spoke as Steve drove us down to the baptism. I was rehearsing my kiss-up speech.

***

Steve got a good spot in the first row of parking. As I helped him lug his camera gear down to the beach I tried to spot Farrah. So far, no sign of her.

"Do you know exactly where we're supposed to meet?" I said.

"She said she'd be on the opposite side from Pavilions, near the lifeguard shack. That would be about where we're standing now."

"Since she's got a bunch of kids to corral she's probably running a little late," I said. In the spirit of 'it's Farrah's big day' I wouldn't dream of mentioning she hadn't been on time for much of anything since the third grade.

Hatch's truck pulled into view. When he parked, it was like watching a clown act as more and more people climbed out. First Farrah and the baby got out of the cab. They were followed by Hatch and a fireman friend of his. Then the twins' mother emerged dragging a diaper bag. In the open bed of the truck, Rain and Echo began climbing out over the sides. Farrah went to help, but she had her hands full with Moke.

I ran over and unlatched the tailgate. Hatch came up behind me.

"Uh, thanks," he said. "I've got it." He plucked one little girl and then the other from the truck bed.

They scampered off and he turned to me. "Wow, I'd almost forgotten what you look like. Did your chauffeur drop you off?"

"Please don't start," I said. "Today is so important to Farrah. Can we can talk later?"

"Fine by me. But who knows? Donald Trump may show up and, uh, trump me. Do you and 'the Donald' have any financial tips you want to share with a lowly hose jockey?" He smiled, but there was more hurt in his voice than humor.

"Okay, I'd hoped we could talk about this later, but I'll give you the punch line now. I'm not taking the money. I've got seven brothers and sisters who want it a heckuva lot more than I do."

"Is it really thirty mil?"

"No, more like ten or twelve. But the will's in probate and the estate's got to be liquidated so it'll take months, maybe a year, to know how much."

"Then what's the rush? Maybe you should wait and see how you feel when it's a done deal before you go giving it away."

"That's why I didn't say anything. I don't want to feel pressured to—"

Steve yelled that he needed us for pictures and I waved. "Be right there."

I turned to Hatch. "Before this gets underway, I want to apologize one more time for missing your awards banquet," I said. "I got so caught up with my family stuff, I haven't been able to think straight."

"No need to apologize. I'm sorry if I acted like a jerk. And I'm real sorry about what happened to your mom. It sucks."

"It does."

"Did you find out any more?" he said.

"Yeah. I'll tell you about it later."

He leaned in and kissed my forehead. "Okay, you got it. But now we've got to go smile for the camera. This is Farrah and Shadow's day."

"Shadow? Oh yeah, I'd forgotten her name."

"She probably made it up," he said. "But I've noticed around here that bogus names are the norm rather than the exception."

Touché, Mr. Decker.

A huge crowd gathered on the beach and a *kahuna* arrived to give the blessing. The guy had to weigh two-fifty, maybe three hundred, pounds. When he finished, he announced it was time for the baptism. Farrah and Shadow followed him to the waterline. He reached down and dipped his hand in the surf and turned toward the twins. The little girls' eyes were locked on each other as the *kahuna* trickled drops on their heads and chanted in Hawaiian. He turned to Shadow and she clarified which name went with each girl. The *kahuna* nodded and repeated the names while the girls hid behind their hands trying to conceal giggles.

Then it was Farrah's turn. She was wearing her favorite billowy lavender caftan. As she clutched the baby on the windswept beach it seemed as if she might get caught in a gust and become airborne like the kite-surfers out on the horizon.

Once again the *kahuna* chanted and put his hand in the surf. He dribbled water on the baby's head while saying his name. Moke's eyes went wide from the shock of the cold water but he didn't make a sound.

The crowd whistled and applauded and the *kahuna* thanked everyone for coming. Then Hatch invited the entire crowd over to his place for beer and food.

***

When the keg was empty and the last of the stragglers had headed home, I started picking up trash and stuffing it in black plastic bags. Steve had driven Farrah and Moke to her apartment and Shadow and the girls had gone to bed in Hatch's guest bedroom.

I was tying off a bag when I felt strong arms encircling me from behind.

"I sure hope this is Hatch," I said, "Because I'm not in the mood for a *big kahuna* love blessing tonight."

He laughed. "Hey, don't knock it 'til you try it."

I turned and looked into his face. It felt so good to gaze into those familiar warm brown eyes and take in that cocky grin. "I've missed you," I said.

"I've missed you too. You know, I have a houseful of girls but I've never felt more alone."

"Maybe it's because half of your 'girls' were under five, and the other half were busy being mommys."

"Could be. I like family life, but this past week it wasn't *my* family. You know what I'm saying?"

I nodded.

"So, we're good?" I said. "I mean, I know I've been neglecting you lately but ever since we went to Kaua'i it's been one thing after another."

He took the trash bag out of my hand and put an arm around my shoulder. "We're good. C'mon, let's go sit on the *lanai*. I've got work in the morning, but I'd like you to catch me up on everything."

I told him about Peggy getting drunk and dying in a car wreck. I told him when I went over to get my birth certificate I'd learned my mom and dad had been married. Then I launched into the full story about how my mom died.

"So, this thirty-year-old your dad married knew the whole story?" he said.

"Apparently. I guess at the end my dad felt bad about everything. I mean, he never got in touch with me. And he married the sister of the guy who killed my mom. The whole situation is weird."

"At least now you know," he said.

"Well, I don't know everything. I know AJ was involved, but who was the other guy?"

"Does it matter? It doesn't change the outcome."

"True," I said. "But as you know, there's no statute of limitations on murder. If I can find the other guy I may have a witness."

"Yeah, but be careful. You're talking about a killer and a reluctant witness. Don't expect the guilty party to come clean, and don't expect the witness to talk, even after all this time."

He slapped his hands on his knees. "But hey, enough about that. Do you want to see my rookie award?"

He went in the house and brought out a citation written in fine calligraphy. It bore an official-looking gold seal and it was framed in an expensive-looking koa-wood frame.

"Wow, this didn't come out of a computer," I said.

"Nope, it's the real deal. I wish you could've been there. It was great. If I ever had second thoughts about switching careers, I don't anymore."

I hugged him. "I'm so proud of you. I'm sorry my messy life got in the way of me being there."

"Yeah, well just so you're there when I make fire chief. I'll order Cristal champagne, and I'm gonna put it on your tab." He laughed.

"About the money—"

The screen door creaked open and Shadow came out on the porch. She wore a clingy tissue-thin camisole, red bikini underpants, and a scowl. She stepped in front of Hatch and crossed her arms but it was too late for me to erase the image of her high firm breasts and erect nipples. "Hatch, don't you have to be at work in the morning?"

"Uh, I guess." He looked over at me. Even in the feeble glow of the porch light I spotted the shame in his eyes.

"Well, then I think you'd better come to bed," she said. She reached out and touched a fingertip to his lips. "I've been waiting."

She shot me a smug look and then flounced back inside the house.

"I better go," I said. I was up and off the lanai in four strides.

Hatch got up. "Hey, I'm sorry you saw that. She promised me she'd cool it when you were here. But I can't—"

"Do us both a favor, Hatch, and go inside. I'll get a ride home from Steve."

"But Pali…"

I was already halfway to the gate.

27

As I worked the keypad on the gate, I heard the screen door slam. I called Steve. Since it was Saturday night I was pretty sure he'd probably gone to the Ball and Chain after dropping off Farrah.

"Hey, Pali," he said, answering just before it would've gone to voicemail.

I stuttered out his name. My throat was barely allowing enough air to pass to speak.

"Are you okay?" he said. "Can you hear me?"

"Yeah," I managed. "Would you mind picking me up?"

"Where are you?"

"At Hatch's."

"And Hatch can't take you home because…?" He seemed to put two and two together pretty fast. "Uh-oh, did something bad happen?"

"Yep," I said.

"I'm leaving right now."

"Thanks. I'll be outside by the gate."

I paced along the ornate wrought-iron gate outside the compound. After what seemed like a half-mile of pacing, I saw the headlights on Steve's Jetta come into view. The lights looked smeary. I guess I'd been crying.

"What happened?" said Steve.

"I found out why Hatch was so eager to take in Shadow."

"What?"

I told him about Shadow slinking out on the lanai and Hatch admitting they'd been sleeping together.

"He came right out and owned up?"

"He said he'd told her to 'cool it' when I was around. And then he acted guilty as hell that he'd gotten caught."

"Wow, that sure doesn't sound like Boy Scout Hatch. I mean, a homeless teenager with three kids?" said Steve. "Yikes."

"Well, technically she just has two kids now since she's handed Moke over to Farrah. Hatch told me he was enjoying 'family life.' And, you know, maybe I'm partially to blame. I haven't been much of a girlfriend for the past couple of weeks."

"OMG, listen to yourself. Don't even try to get me to believe you think this is okay, because it's not. For a whole raft of reasons."

"Yeah, but we both know how much Hatch loves to save people," I said. "Why do you think they made him Rookie of the Year?"

***

I woke up on Sunday and it took me a minute to remember what'd happened the night before. I headed to the kitchen for coffee before even running a brush through my hair.

"Uh-oh, looks like someone's already letting herself go," said Steve. "Here." He handed me a huge mug of black coffee.

"Cream? Sugar?" I said.

"It's just fat and carbs, hon. You really need to steer clear of that stuff now that you're back on the market."

I pushed him aside and rummaged through the refrigerator. I grabbed the creamer and slammed it down on the counter.

"Excuse me, I need to get to the sugar," I said, wagging a finger at the cabinet behind him. "I'd suggest you step aside. This is not a good morning to get between me and my vices."

He took a giant step sideways. "I predict in six months you'll have ten million reasons you'll be glad you're rid of Hatch Decker. Maybe more."

"Don't take any bets on that because, more than ever, I've decided there's no way I'm taking that money. You know what they say, money changes everything."

"Oh yeah, like you couldn't use a few changes in your life? How about getting a decent set of wheels? That thing you call a car is more rust than metal. And how great would it be to pay off this house and not sweat the mortgage every month? Think about it, Pali, you could buy a new house. An enormous mansion down at the beach."

"I don't want an enormous mansion. I want things to go back to the way they were. Before I found out my dad was a rich jerk and my mom was bashed in the head with a baseball bat. I should never have gone to Kaua'i. I should've done like wife number five and just not shown up."

Steve rubbed his thumb and fingertips together. "You may not realize it now, but if you'll just allow yourself to embrace the Paris Hilton lifestyle I'm sure you'd come to love it. It's time to let go of the old to make room for the new."

I dragged myself back to the bathroom for a shower. I'd convinced myself I didn't want Phil's money, but maybe Steve had a point. A fresh start. I liked the sound of that.

***

After a slovenly Sunday I made myself go to work on Monday. I might be an 'heiress-in-waiting' but the 'in-waiting' part reminded me I still needed to book a few weddings for the foreseeable future.

I fiddled around on my website and put up an ad offering a twenty-percent discount to couples who booked within the next month. It took me longer than I'd expected and soon my stomach was growling. I saved the changes and went next door to the Gadda to get something to eat. I considered grabbing a yogurt, then nixed that idea. Nope, what I wanted was some Little Debbie's. I hadn't eaten a Little Debbie's Devil Square since college. We used to call them 'dorm crack.'

As usual, Farrah was busy with a customer when I came in. She had Moke crammed into a baby sling across her breast, and although I'd never say it, she looked kind of kangaroo-ish. I waited until she was free and then I plunked a white box of Devil Squares on the counter.

"You sure you don't want to reconsider?" she said. "You know, they don't call them 'Devil' Squares for nothing."

"One-hundred-percent sure."

"Well, do you have a permission slip from Sifu Doug? I don't want him calling the cops and accusing me of aiding and abetting."

"Just ring 'em up, okay?"

She punched in the sale on her ancient cash register and then hesitated before handing over my change.

"Something's wrong, isn't it? she said. "Is it Hatch?"

"You're the psychic."

She glowered at me.

"Okay, I really don't want to get into it, but it seems Hatch is having a fling with Shadow."

"No way."

"Way." I told her about Shadow modeling her lingerie for us on Saturday night.

"That doesn't mean anything."

"She ordered him to come to bed. Said she was waiting for him. And then he apologized by saying he'd told her to 'cool it' when I was around."

Farrah bit her lip. "I'll get to the bottom of this. I promise."

I took my Little Debbie booty back to my shop, hoping to pass the afternoon in a chocolate and sugar haze. The mail had been pushed through the mail slot and I picked it up. I ripped the plastic wrap off a Devil Square and started munching while I sorted the catalogs and brochures from the few pieces of first class mail. There were two white envelopes. One had the Hawaii Department of Vital Records as the return address. I slit it open, then wiped my sticky hands on a tissue before removing what was inside.

Each of the two pages in the envelope bore the Hawaii State Seal. The top sheet was my mother's death certificate. It was typed in all caps, which made it feel like someone was shouting. My breathing gave a little hitch when I noted the date and time she'd been pronounced, and then it hitched again when I read the cause of death—cerebral hemorrhage.

"True," I whispered. "But not the whole truth, so help me God."

I thought about how, sooner or later, I was going to have to call Jeff and tell him what I'd learned. That our mom had been brutally murdered and justice had been denied her for over thirty years. I wasn't looking forward to that conversation.

The second sheet was my mom's marriage certificate. It was on light green safety paper with a watermark to help detect copies or forgeries. I was startled to read the date and realize she'd been married just weeks before she died. But then I read further. I read and re-read one line since it seemed my eyes were playing tricks on me. Then I dropped the certificate on the desk and stared out the window.

Like it or not, I had to go back to Kaua'i.

28

I called the airlines and booked a flight for the next morning. I'd be taking a carry-on bag because this time I wouldn't be coming home until I'd cut through all the lies. Then I called Sunny.

"I've got a few days off and I'd like to come for a visit," I said. "Is it okay if I stay at your place?"

"You're always welcome," she said, but her tone was wary. "When were you planning to come?"

"Tomorrow." I figured I better offer some explanation. "Yeah, things with my boyfriend are kind of tense. I thought maybe a few days apart might help."

"When are you arriving? I'll send Timo down to get you."

"*Mahalo*, but I think I'll rent a car. I'd like to take some drives; maybe go to the beach for an afternoon."

"Suit yourself."

I folded up my mother's death and marriage certificates and slipped them in my purse. Then I locked up the shop and drove home. No sense hanging around pretending I was working. My mind was already on Kaua'i.

***

On Tuesday morning I caught the eight-fifteen direct into Lihue. I rented the most inconspicuous car on the lot—a silver-gray Ford Focus. Before going to Sunny's I stopped at the police station on Ka'ana Street.

A handsome wet-behind-the-ears duty clerk greeted me and asked what he could do for me. I considered a politically incorrect remark but stifled it. If I was going to get what I'd come for, I needed to play it straight.

"I'm here about an incident that happened thirty years ago," I said. "On the North Shore."

"That was a long time ago."

We held each other's gaze and I was pretty sure he was thinking what I was thinking, *before he was even born*.

"I know. But I'm not talking about a parking ticket or littering," I said. "I'm here regarding an unsolved murder."

He sat up straighter. "Okay. Then you should probably talk to a detective."

He looked down at his console and punched in some numbers. Then he turned in his chair so he no longer faced me and spoke quietly into his headset. Did he think I could read lips? Or maybe he was telling them he had a nutcase out front. After a few back and forths with the person on the other end he swiveled back around.

"Sorry. I forgot to ask your name."

"Pali Moon."

He returned to his nearly inaudible conversation and after another half-minute he returned with a verdict. "Detective Wong says she can be back here in fifteen to twenty minutes. She'd like you to wait."

I took a seat in the all-beige waiting room. People refer to cops as the 'thin blue line' but in my experience, beige is the operative color.

Half-an-hour later, Detective Kiki Wong came into the waiting room from somewhere in the back. She led me to the same nondescript interview room I'd been in when I'd been questioned about Peggy Chesterton's accident. She pointed to a seat at the table and then sat across from me. The room was spooky quiet. All I could hear was the low *shush* of the air conditioner fan.

"Sorry to make you wait. We're working a burglary in Nawiliwili."

"Any news on the Peggy Chesterton accident?" I said.

"Not much. Are you here to enlighten me?" She perked up, as if hoping I was there to unburden my soul and fill in the blanks.

"No, sorry. I'm here about a cold case."

She squinted, as if getting ready to blow me off with, '*Not my job.*'

"I think the Kaua'i Police Department was involved in covering up a brutal murder in 1981," I said. Nothing like leading with a sharp jab.

"That's a pretty serious allegation," she said.

"Yeah, well it's a pretty serious offense."

"What leads you to believe this, Ms. Moon?"

"My mother lived in Hanalei in 1981 and on the night of April 16, 1981 she was beaten to death. The police called it an accident. They didn't even investigate it."

"Are you sure about that?"

"What? Am I sure my mother was beaten to death? Or sure the police didn't investigate?"

"Both," she said. She leaned back in her chair. I had a hunch she'd much rather have been dealing with the burglary in Nawiliwili.

I pulled out my mom's death certificate and slid it across the table. Then I told Wong the story I'd heard from both Joanie Bush and Sunny Wilkerson. She listened, but hardly lifted her eyes from the certificate.

"Is that it?" she said when I finished.

"Isn't that enough?" I'd implicated AJ Chesterton, big-time, and from where I was sitting it looked as if she was struggling to decide what to do with my allegations.

"I'd like to take this one step at a time. Let me make a copy of the death certificate and see what I come up with regarding this incident. Obviously I wasn't on the force at the time and many of the people who were are retired." I figured she was referring to AJ's father, Arthur Chesterton. The Chestertons had just held Peggy's memorial service so the timing was about as lousy as it could be.

"Are you staying on the island?" she said.

"Yes. Up at Sunny Wilkerson's," I said.

"Good. We'll be in touch."

She led me out to the lobby. As I was about to go outside, she said, "Oh, and Miss Moon? I'd prefer you keep this to yourself for now. The Chestertons are...well, you can imagine."

I nodded.

I drove up to Sunny's. She remotely opened the gate and I made my way through the thick foliage. As the branches scraped the sides of the rental car I once again felt as if I was being watched. It was the same feeling I'd had up at Taylor Camp. Creepy, but somehow encouraging at the same time. Like when Farrah talks about communing with her guardian angel.

Sunny came out to greet me. "Did you have trouble finding the place on your own? I was beginning to worry. I expected you an hour ago."

"Oh, sorry. I stopped off at the police station," I said.

"Why?"

"I wanted to talk to the police."

"About?"

"About my mother's death."

"Oh Pali. Let it go. It was such a long time ago. I'm sure your mother would want you to—"

"I doubt if you have the slightest idea what my mother would want. Getting to the bottom of this is as much for me and my brother as for my mother. We want to know what happened."

"Suit yourself. Why don't you take your things to the *ohana* and come back and join me for a glass of sun tea?"

I parked in front of the guest house. When I went inside I felt like calling Sunny and telling her I needed an hour to freshen up and then tearing the place apart looking for—what? I had to make do with testing her reaction to the evidence I already had.

When I went over to the main house Sunny was outside waiting for me. I sat down and she handed me a glass of sun tea.

"This is good," I said, taking a sip.

"It's my personal blend. I get it at an organic tea shop in Waipouli. So, tell me what's going on," she said. "I can't believe the police had much to say after all these years."

"My father's name was Philip James Wilkerson, right?

"That's right. Well, technically, Philip James Wilkerson, *the Third*. He was named after his father and grandfather. I guess when he was little everyone called him 'PJ'. He hated that."

"And what was his brother's name?"

"Robert. Phil said his brother was named for your mother's father."

"Robert Allen?"

"Yes, I think that's right." She narrowed her eyes. "Why do you ask?"

I pulled out the certificates I'd received from Vital Records and handed her the marriage certificate. She took it, gave it a quick glance and then dropped it on the table between us.

"Huh. Well, I guess now you know," she said.

"My mother was married to my uncle?"

"It was kind of a mess," she said.

"I'm sure. But I want to know."

"Okay, as you already know, Phil and your mother lived up at Taylor Camp in the mid-70's. Right after you were born he ran out of money and his father made him come home and go to college. He promised your mom he'd come back after he finished. He told me he wrote to her while he was gone but she never wrote back.

"So, anyway, when he graduated from the University of Oregon he came back to Kaua'i. By that time Taylor Camp had been burned down and everybody had moved. He found your mom living in an *ohana* on some other woman's property."

"My Auntie Mana?"

"He didn't say. Anyway, when your dad came back…" she stopped and chewed on her lower lip. In the silence that followed I picked up the fragrance of a nearby plumeria tree.

"Don't stop now," I said. "What happened when he came back?"

"Are you sure you want to hear this? I mean, when Phil told me I thought maybe the drugs were messing with his head or something."

"Go on."

She blew out a breath. "Okay, so your dad comes back and finds your mom. But by then she had another kid. He couldn't believe it."

"My brother, Jeff."

"Yeah. Trouble was, it was also his brother's."

"Okay, you lost me there."

"Your mother had hooked up with Robert, your father's brother, while Phil was away at school."

"So, Uncle Robby really *was* my uncle?"

"I guess so. Robert had come to Kaua'i to visit Phil after he got out of the Army. When Phil went back to Oregon, Robert told him he was moving to Honolulu to look for a job, but he didn't. He stayed. Then Phil showed back up."

I was trying to put the pieces together but some didn't fit.

"Okay, so my mom started living with Phil's brother after my dad left for college?"

"Yeah, but Phil thought she didn't know."

"Didn't know what? Didn't know that Robert was Phil's brother?"

"No, of course she knew that. Phil thought she didn't know he was planning to come back. Phil said he sent his letters General Delivery to the Hanalei Post Office. And he said Robert must've intercepted his letters to your mom."

I squinted. "That's just weird. Why would he do that?"

"Who knows? The guy had been wounded in Vietnam. He had a drug problem. Phil invited him to come over to Kaua'i to relax and get his head on straight. It never dawned on him his own brother would put the moves on his girlfriend."

"Why did Phil think Robert had taken the mail?"

"Because after Robert died, Phil found the letters. He said Robert had hidden them."

"So, Phil and Robert got in a fight?"

"Yeah. Phil said a few nights after he came back to Kaua'i his brother sneaked in his room while he was sleeping. Robert was drunk or high or something and he made so much noise crashing into the room that it woke Phil up. Robert was carrying a baseball bat." Sunny took a sip of tea. "What happened that night haunted your dad 'til his dying day."

I shot her a skeptical look.

"Anyway, Robert took a swing at Phil but he was so messed up he missed. Right about then your mom showed up and tried to break it up. I guess when Robert raised the bat again, your mom was in the way."

I put my hands up to cover my mouth. They were ice cold.

"Uncle Robby killed my mom?"

"I'm afraid so."

"And then…" I knew what was coming.

"And then he killed himself," she said. "Phil tried to stop him, but it was too late."

29

I was in the *ohana* when my phone rang. The caller ID said, *Unavailable*, but cops don't want you to know they're calling so I wasn't surprised when it turned out to be Detective Wong.

"Am I catching you at a bad time?" she said.

"No, it's fine." I said. Actually, I couldn't recall a worse time, but there was no turning back. I was eager to hear if Wong had found anything to verify Sunny's bizarre story.

"I did a records search and found the incident report. My boss says he's willing to let you take a look at it."

"Can I get a copy?"

"No, the file stays here. But if you'll come in, you can go through it."

I left the compound without telling Sunny. It was weird enough having a step-mother five years younger than me; no way would I play the role of step-child.

I drove to the Lihue police station. The same hunky desk jockey was at the front. I wondered if the guy was a street cop who'd messed up and was doing penance.

"You're here for Detective Wong, right?" he said.

I thought the Wong/right thing was funny but had a hunch he wouldn't see the humor.

"Yeah."

Kiki Wong took me to the interview room and set a thin manila file folder in front of me.

"This is it?" I said. I'd expected a big white box like you see on TV. I mean, after all, it involved a killing—accidental or not.

"There wasn't much to report. The investigating officer ruled it an accidental death. And then the alleged assailant committed suicide. Seems he jumped from Kalalau." She shrugged, then seemed to realize how disrespectful that looked and said, "Look, I'm sorry. I know this is regarding your mother. Take your time, but please leave everything in the same order you found it."

She left and I flipped the file folder open. The first few pages included the final incident report, typewritten and stapled together. In narrative form, it described the arrival of the police, the subsequent arrival of an ambulance, and the later search for the alleged attacker. It ended by saying an eyewitness had observed a man fall from a cliff off above the Kalalau trailhead, and when the body was recovered it was later identified as the alleged assailant.

The second set of stapled papers included the witness reports. There were notes from interviews with Auntie Mana—who was referred to by her real name, Maliana Kahele—as well as two other people whose names I didn't recognize. The witnesses seemed to corroborate Sunny's story. They'd heard a fight between two men, and called the police. When the police arrived, they found my mother gravely injured in the *ohana*. The men were gone, but no one witnessed them leaving.

After that came the autopsy report. I wasn't ready to delve into that in great detail. There was an outline drawing of the body with marks I assumed indicated wounds. The pathologist had used a larger line drawing of a human head to pinpoint the location of the fatal hemorrhage.

I leafed through the rest of the file but didn't see anything of interest. I did notice there were establishing shots of the *ohana* and the yard outside, but no photos of my mother's body or even the murder scene itself and I thought that was odd.

I shut the file and took it to the front desk. The guy asked me to wait while he called Detective Wong. When I handed her the file, she nodded but didn't say anything.

"Don't you want to check to make sure it's all there?" I said.

"I will. But I trust you." Seemed to me one thing cancelled out the other, but again, I kept it to myself. Who knows how much trouble she'd had getting her boss to agree to let me see it?

"I have a question," I said.

"Certainly." She looked down at the desk clerk. "Would you like to talk in private?"

"No, that's not necessary. I just want to know why there's no mention of the two men's names."

"I'm not following."

"In all the reports and interviews no one says who the guys involved in the fight might be. Doesn't that seem odd?"

"Sorry, I don't have an answer for you. I'll be honest. You probably noticed we cleaned up the file a little. For instance, there are no crime scene shots or photos of the victim. No sense in you seeing those. But beyond that, as far as I know, this is the entire incident report."

"Sunny Wilkerson told me that before my father died, he admitted he'd been there. He claimed he'd been the intended target."

"Well, according to this, he was gone by the time the police arrived."

"But nobody asked? I mean, even if he wasn't there, wouldn't the responding officer ask if someone was staying in the *ohana*? Don't you think people would at least speculate who it was? I mean, really. We're talking Hanalei, not New York."

"Witnesses are often unreliable. And, from what I was told, back in the eighties there were clashes between certain North Shore residents and the police. My best guess is no one was willing to name names."

I thanked her and went out to my car. I sat there trying to decide where to go next. Once again I felt the same weird sensation of someone watching me. I twisted around and checked the back seat. Empty. Then I got out and went back inside the police station.

I told the desk clerk I had one more question for Detective Wong. He shot me a little *stink eye* before calling her back out front.

"I'm sorry to bother you again," I said to Wong. "But after all that, I didn't make a note of the name of the officer who prepared the report. I guess I was so busy reading the account I overlooked it."

She asked the desk clerk to unlock the wooden gate separating the lobby from the working area of the station. He buzzed her through and she touched my elbow, signaling I should walk with her.

After we got outside and the glass door had closed behind us she said, "It was Chief Chesterton."

"Arthur Chesterton?"

"Yes."

"I wonder how much Peggy knew about this," I said.

"Well, you certainly can't ask her now," said Wong. "But maybe Mayor Chesterton remembers more than is in the report."

"I thought he had Alzheimer's or something."

"I don't think so. I spoke with him briefly at Peggy's memorial and he seemed okay. He was devastated, of course, but he managed to hold his own. *Hundreds* of people came to pay their respects." She held my gaze. I wasn't sure if the stare-down was to shame me for not showing up at my father's ex-wife's memorial or because she still thought I had something to do with Peggy's death.

"Do you know where I might find him?"

"I can't promise he knows anything, or even if he'd be willing to talk to you if he does, but last I heard he was down at Garden Island Manor. It's an assisted living place."

"*Mahalo.*"

I drove to Garden Island Manor. From the outside, it looked like a cheery apartment building with a new paint job, carefully manicured landscaping, and a little flock of colorful Kaua'i chickens pecking contentedly in the flower beds. But once I stepped inside it felt more like a fortress than a residence.

There was a woman behind a desk guarding the entrance. Her name badge said, 'Joy.' She had frizzy red hair and her face looked like a gargoyle, one of those scary mythical creatures with buggy eyes and a pointy chin. In medieval days, builders positioned carved gargoyles on the eaves of buildings to scare away intruders. This real-life version seemed to be performing the same task.

"Sorry," she said when I asked if she'd call Arthur Chesterton's room. "I don't believe we have a resident by that name."

"Would you at least check your residents' list? I'm pretty sure he's here. A detective at the police station told me I'd find him here."

"We do not give out personal information regarding our residents," she said.

"I'm not asking for his mother's maiden name," I said. "I just want to see if he'll talk with me."

"We only allow visitors on Tuesdays, Thursdays and Sundays."

"Then I guess it's my lucky day, because today is Tuesday."

She glanced at the page-a-day calendar on her desk and scowled as she turned the page to the correct date.

"But are you expected? Our residents deserve and require a certain level of security. We can't just let in anybody."

"I'm only asking you to call him. We can meet here in the lobby if he's concerned about his safety."

She deepened her scowl. "I will allow you to leave a written message for the mayor. If he wants to see you, he'll let me know." I found it amusing that everyone still referred to Arthur Chesterton as "the mayor" even though he hadn't been in office for a dozen years or more.

"So, I guess he *does* live here," I said.

She shot me a *don't push your luck* look as she handed over a notepad and pencil.

I wrote a note asking Arthur Chesterton to call if he'd be willing to see me. I signed it, and under my name I wrote 'Philip Wilkerson's daughter.'

I'd made it halfway back to Sunny's when my phone rang. The caller ID read, *A Chesterton*.

I pulled over to take the call. After I answered, a reedy male voice said, "Phil warned me you were smart. Seems he was right."

30

Arthur Chesterton advised me he'd be going to dinner in a little while so if I wanted to see him I needed to get there *wiki wiki*. The clock on the dash showed three forty-five. I made it back to Garden Island Manor in less than twenty minutes. When I came through the door I gave the gargoyle an engaging smile, but she wasn't having any of it.

"So, Joy, seems the mayor is really looking forward to my visit," I said.

"Don't flatter yourself. These old farts run out to talk to the meter reader."

I signed in and she pulled out a yellow plastic 'visitor' badge on a lanyard. "You've got to display this on your person at all times."

I told her the mayor had said he'd be in the music room and I asked where that was. She pointed a hooked thumb toward a hallway on the other side of the lobby.

I walked down a closed-in hall that smelled like Shalimar perfume and laundry soap. At the end was a large room, painted an industrial shade of green and sporting a shiny speckled vinyl floor. Inside, a stooped man with a fringe of white hair was playing an electric organ. He leaned in toward the keyboard and then back out again as if he were on a rolling ship. His eyes were closed.

"Excuse me," I said, interrupting an especially ambitious section featuring lots of chord changes with the left hand and his right hand fingers rapidly moving up and down the keys.

He lifted his hands from the keyboard and opened his eyes, blinking in the bluish glare of the fluorescent lights as if waking from a deep sleep.

"Do you play?" he said.

"No. I took *ukulele* lessons in school, but I never mastered much beyond "My Dog Has Fleas"."

He shook his head. "Don't know that one."

"That's okay. I don't recognize what you were just playing, either."

"Scott Joplin. *The Entertainer*," he said. "Sounds better on a piano."

"Sorry to interrupt, but you mentioned you'll be to dinner soon."

"That's fine. I have a good idea why you're here. I'd hoped to be long dead, but first it took Phil and then my Peggy. Seems like some kind of comeuppance, you know?"

I didn't have a clue what he was talking about. Maybe the old guy did have dementia.

"Mayor Chesterton, like I said on the note, I'm Phil Wilkerson's oldest daughter."

"I know; I can read. I may be old but I'm not illiterate. Phil told me about you. He said he regretted never meeting you."

"My mother told me he left after I was born. I guess he saw me when I was a baby."

"Ah, yes. But that's not the same, is it? Babies are all alike. It's when they grow up that you get to see what you've created. Good or bad."

"*Ohana*," I said.

"Yes, that's right, *ohana*."

"If you wouldn't mind," I said. "I'd really appreciate it if you'd tell me what you remember about that night."

He hung his head. At first I was afraid it meant he couldn't remember. But then I realized he simply wasn't looking forward to talking about it.

"It's been a long time," he said.

"Thirty years."

"You better take a seat," he said, gesturing toward a folding chair. "This could take a while."

I dragged a gray metal chair over next to the organ bench. "Are you comfortable there?" I said. "Do you want me to get you a chair?"

"No matter where I sit I won't be comfortable talking about this." He took a deep breath and then released a series of dry coughs. "I'd only been police chief for about two months when a call comes in about a domestic disturbance up in Hanalei. It wasn't unusual. There were a lot of drugs up there. We sort of let them be. If we'd try to bust every hippie for every little sack of *pakalolo* we wouldn't have had time to do anything else."

Another deep breath, another series of coughs.

"The island was different then. Everybody knew everybody. And everyone knew their place. My *ohana* got along okay. We were *haole*-looking, like you, but we'd been here since the plantation days. My father worked sugar up in Kilauea. He rose through the ranks until he was in charge of a big operation up there. But he never owned nuthin'. Never owned a house or a car. His whole life he knew he'd never be more than a hard-workin' company man."

Again, a few coughs, deeper this time.

"Anyhow, so this call comes in about a DD up north. I was just leaving a meeting up in Princeville, so I called in and said I'd take the domestic. Every so often, I liked to take a call. You know, there's just so much paperwork you can do before you stop feeling like a cop. When I get to the incident address, I see a guy standing outside. He's holding a baseball bat and he looks all wild in the eyes and like that.

"The neighbors were nowhere to be seen. Prob'ly the bat scared 'em off or they didn't want to get involved. I don't blame 'em. I had no idea what had happened or what the dude was thinkin'. I know I was thinkin' I shoulda called for back-up."

"Did you recognize the man?" I said.

"Nope. I was familiar with most everyone on the island; even a lot of those hippie-types up there, but I couldn't remember ever seeing the guy before. Anyhow, I talked him into handing over the bat and then he started cryin' and actin' all sorry and all that.

A few more coughs. "I asked him to tell me what happened and he pointed to a little *ohana* out back. We went in and I saw two people on the floor—a man and a woman. Neither was movin'. Even so, I use my radio to call for a bus, you know, an ambulance. I turn around and see the guy's on the damn phone. Now, two things come to mind. First, I'm the chief of police, and I've let a perp out of my sight for long enough to make a phone call? And, second, who was this kid calling? His lawyer?

Arthur went on. "So, I go over to snap on the cuffs and he pushes the phone at me and says, '*My father wants to talk to you.*' To my dying day I won't know why I took that phone.

Arthur was wracked by a long bout of coughing. When it ended, he pulled out a balled-up handkerchief and wiped his mouth. "Sorry. I've had a cold for a while now."

I waited.

"And here's where it goes bad," he said. "Here's where I come to that fork in the road you hear about."

This time when he stopped talking he didn't cough. Instead, he scrubbed his face with his hands. "I take the phone and the guy's father said something I've never forgotten."

We locked eyes.

"He said, *I already lost one son. I'll do anything if you'll help me not lose them both.* By then, I knew the ambulance was on its way. I had to think fast."

He stopped and looked at me as if giving me time to put the pieces together. "Phil Wilkerson was the guy with the bat." I said.

He nodded.

"And his brother, Robert, and my mother, Marta Warner, were the two people on the floor."

He nodded again.

OMG. The picture the puzzle was forming was too horrendous to consider.

Arthur Chesterton continued, "Seems your father had gotten wind that his former girlfriend—your mother—had up and married his brother. He came over to try and win her back, or anyway that's what he told me, but he ended up killing them both instead."

I couldn't breathe. It was as if someone had clamped a hand over my nose and mouth and gut-punched me at the same time.

"But Sunny told me…" I said.

"Who knows what she knows? Phil didn't come clean to many people. He told my Peggy, because, what the hell, she wouldn't say nuthin'. Her old man was as guilty as him, maybe more."

"Did Phil push Robert's body off the cliff?"

Arthur nodded, "And I helped him. Even drove him up there."

"But what about the ambulance?"

"We'd headed out before they got there. I radioed I was chasing down the alleged assailant, who'd taken off."

"Why?"

"I already told you why. The old man wanted me to protect Phil."

"I meant why did you agree to cover this up? You were the chief of police."

"I was. But I wanted more. For my kids, my *ohana*. I wanted to be mayor."

"And Phil's father helped you?"

"He sent me three times more money than I needed for the campaign. And every year on the anniversary, I'd get a nice check in the mail."

"Who came up with the story of Robert coming in with the bat?"

"That was Phil. While we were on our way up to Kalalau, he figured it out. He wanted to say he'd wrestled the bat away and had killed in self-defense, but how did that make sense with two people down? And, I was worried about the forensics. We had to get rid of the bat."

"And so Robert committed suicide and took the bat with him when he jumped."

I stared at the floor. My breath was coming in strangled gulps and my eyes stung.

Arthur took my hand. I didn't pull it away. "I know what I did was wrong, but where was the hurt? I saved your father from prison and then his father saved me from a second-rate life."

"You don't believe that," I said.

"I don't anymore. But that's what I told myself for years. When Phil asked if he could marry Peggy, you can imagine what I thought. I knew he'd killed before, and I worried about her every day. But it wasn't as if I could say anything. And for what, twelve or thirteen years, they got along fine. Then he met that other gal and broke Peggy's heart."

"But Sunny said you all kept in touch."

"Oh, you bet I did. You know what they say, about keeping your friends close and your enemies closer? Phil and I had a bond. It's strange, but I grew to love him like a son. AJ used to throw fits over Phil always hanging around."

"When I first heard about my mother being killed I thought AJ killed her."

"No, AJ's never loved a woman enough to do that."

A cold shiver made me rub my arms. "I need to let you get to your dinner."

"*Mahalo* for coming to see me," he said. "I'm sorry about your mother. I'm afraid by the time I got there it was already too late. I hope you understand why I did what I did."

I would never understand but there was no use spitting in his face. I thanked him and went outside to my car. Then I put my head in my hands and cried.

31

When I finished crying, I wiped my face on my shirt sleeve and got back on the road to Sunny's. I felt a white-hot flame in my chest that would only be extinguished by watching her squirm when I revealed how her precious Phil had been not only a liar but a murderer. And not just any murderer. He'd not only killed the mother of his child, but his own brother. As painful as it was to think about, I couldn't help but pray Phil had killed my mother first, sparing her the anguish of watching her husband suffer and knowing her own fate was sealed.

I had to keep looking down at the speedometer. I was going over sixty on Kuhio Highway, but it felt like I was merely inching along.

I focused on my breathing. Sifu Doug was big on breath control. He'd had us practice until we nearly passed out. I hated breath training. It was boring. And in a match, when I got on the mat and lifted my head to face my opponent, breath control was usually the last thing on my mind.

But now I was acutely aware of my breathing. It was fast and shallow; the kind Sifu Doug cautioned against. I drew a long breath in through my nose and held it for a count of ten. Then I released it through my mouth, counting to fifteen. After a few controlled breaths I felt a little better. But only a little.

***

I roughed up the rental car as I careened down the bumpy track to Sunny's, but managed to make it to the main house without breaking an axle. She must've heard me coming, because she came out on the lanai and waved. I got out and went up to meet her.

"Have a seat," she said. "Where've you been? I was starting to worry."

"Well, I'm afraid you're not done worrying," I said, taking a seat next to her. It wasn't a great opening salvo but it would have to do. I was too eager to get to the knock-out punch to finesse my words.

She squinted.

"I was just over at Garden Island Manor," I said. "I had a nice chat with your former mayor."

That brought out a big smile. "Phil loved Arthur. Phil told me that after his father died, Arthur treated him like a son." She reached over and patted my knee. "Tell you what, you've been gone all day and I'm sure we have a lot to talk about. Let me get you a mai tai. It's my special recipe."

I hesitated. "I haven't eaten much today. Maybe I'll have one later."

"I've got dinner waiting, so I'll just make it a short one. You look exhausted."

She went in the house and came back carrying two ceramic cups shaped like pineapples. She'd garnished my drink with the obligatory paper umbrella and cherry-on-a-pick.

"Why didn't you give yourself an umbrella?" I said.

"I save those for guests. And those cherries make my tongue itch. Cheers." She held up her cup and we clinked. "Now tell me that's not the best mai tai you've ever tasted."

I took a sip and it was good. A bit on the sweet side, but tasty.

"Your dad taught me how to make these. According to him, Peggy was quite a fan before she stopped drinking."

"Listen, Sunny. I've learned something you need to know from Arthur Chesterton."

"You know, our former mayor lives in a nursing home for a reason."

"It's not a nursing home; it's assisted living."

"Whatever. But the man's not, you know, all there." She tapped her head.

"He seemed 'there' enough to me. He told me Phil went to college but then he came back in 1981 and discovered my mom had another baby and she'd married his brother and he—"

"Sweetie, you're rambling. Drink up so we can go in and have dinner."

I saw something in her eyes that made me change course. "You're right, I'm so tired. Why don't you go on in and I'll finish up?" I said. "I need to wash up first."

"Good," she said. "See you inside."

***

I poured the drink down the bathroom sink. After not eating all day the last thing I needed was a syrupy mai tai. I washed my hands and went into the dining room.

About halfway through dinner the room began to swim. I tried shutting my eyes but when I opened them again everything was in a different spot. I had a hard time gripping the fork and I dropped it at least twice.

"Are you okay?" said Sunny.

"I don't know. My stomach feels a little off."

I'd decided that as much I'd enjoy watching Sunny squirm, I should report Arthur Chesterton's confession to Detective Wong about before I said anything to anyone else. Sunny chattered through dinner and never once asked me to finish telling about my visit with Arthur. As she blathered on, I got the sinking feeling she may already know the truth.

"You look so wiped out," she said. "Let me make you a cup of 'sleep happy' tea while I clean up the dishes. I love the stuff. After Phil died I used to have a cup every night to help with insomnia."

"I don't think insomnia will be a problem," I said." I could fall asleep right here."

"But I want to hear what crazy Arthur told you. Why don't you go on out to the lanai and put your feet up. I'll bring the tea right out."

"Can it wait until tomorrow?" I said. "I'm so exhausted."

She looked annoyed. "Suit yourself."

I staggered to the guest house with my stomach in an uproar. I felt drunk-sick even though I'd had less than half of the mai tai. I flopped down on the sofa. No way could I bring myself to sleep in the murderer's bed.

***

On Wednesday morning the sun was streaming in the windows when I woke up. My stomach felt raw and I had a roaring hangover. Then I remembered my visit with Arthur Chesterton and I made myself get up.

I used the bathroom but it didn't make me feel much better. I splashed water on my face and headed over to the main house. I tried the door, not bothering to knock. When I got inside, I heard Sunny on the phone in the back somewhere. The sound of her voice made my stomach hitch and I felt sick again. I nearly made it to the guest bathroom in time. Nearly, but not quite.

I'm not a sickly person, so vomiting always catches me by surprise. But there it was, on Sunny's spotless bathroom floor. I felt a little better but my stomach still burned. I dragged myself to the kitchen to find something to clean up the mess.

I grabbed the edge of the sink and worked to control my breathing. When I'd regained a bit of composure, I opened the cabinet under the sink to look for a rag.

I moved a few things around and then I saw it. It was a bulky yellow plastic jug with an unfamiliar label. Unfamiliar, but not unknown.

I'd first come across anti-freeze when I was doing my final stint of air marshal training in Atlantic City, New Jersey. A fellow trainee had chided me for not 'winterizing' my car. He'd warned me that when the temperature dropped I'd come out one morning and I'd find my car had become a one-ton paperweight instead of transportation. On the mainland, people keep anti-freeze in their garage all year long. But I could think of no good reason to keep anti-freeze under a kitchen sink in Kaua'i.

I grabbed the jug and went to locate my stepmother.

32

I pushed through the master bedroom door. Sunny was sitting in an armchair wearing a white terry cloth robe. She'd wrapped a bright blue towel around her head and she was chatting on her cell.

"What are you doing barging in like this?" she said, popping up. "As you can see, I'm on the phone." I was holding the anti-freeze jug behind my back, and when I brought it out where she could see it, I watched her eyes widen.

"I gotta go," she said to the caller. Then she threw the phone on the bed.

"Look what I found in the kitchen."

"What are you doing going through my stuff?"

"You liar. You knew all along, didn't you?"

"Don't believe that old man, Pali. It just like I said. Robert started it. Phil just grabbed the bat."

"And clubbed them both to death."

"Look, I promised your father I'd—"

I advanced on her in attack position. "Don't you *ever* refer to that murderer that way again. Philip Wilkerson killed my mother in cold blood."

She stepped back and grabbed a lamp off the nightstand. Then she yanked the cord out of of the wall. "Don't come any closer."

"Why'd you poison Peggy?" I said. "Were you afraid she'd contest the will? Or was she blackmailing you? Threatening to air the Wilkerson's dirty secret unless you threw a few bucks her way?"

"I don't know what you're talking about. Peggy died in a car crash."

"Yeah, after you'd laced her drink with anti-freeze. And then you sent her over to me so I'd be the last person to see her alive."

"You're nuts. All that Homeland Security crap must've turned you paranoid." She parried the lamp toward me as if goading me to try and grab it.

"Put the stupid lamp down," I said.

She threw it against the opposite wall and as my eyes flicked toward the moving object, she reached into the nightstand and pulled out a pistol. It was a small nine millimeter, probably a Kel-Tec PF-9 or maybe a Walther.

"Okay. I don't want to use this," she said pointing the gun at my chest. "But I just need some time to think."

She sidestepped to the bed and picked up her cell phone. "Timo, I need you to bring the car around."

There was a pause and then she said in a tight voice, "No, *right* now."

I watched her bearing like I'd read a martial arts opponent. What were my odds? I ran through the likely scenarios and then acted.

I ducked and Sunny fired. So much for not planning to use it. The shot was not as loud as I'd imagined it'd be, but it was certainly loud enough to bring Timo running. I brought up one leg and caught her square in the sternum. She crashed onto her back, but still somehow managed to keep her grip on the gun.

With Timo on the way, my best recourse was to bolt. There was no way I could hold off both of them. The master bedroom had a door that opened onto the lanai. I figured it would be locked, but I managed to twist the lock open and make it outside before Sunny had a chance to aim.

Blam! I didn't bother to turn around and see where the bullet had gone.

I headed toward my rental car but then remembered the keys were in my purse. Just as I hit the steps of the *ohana*, I heard running footsteps coming up on my right.

Timo.

"Stop right there," he said.

In the split second I had to react, I made my decision. I hit the door of the *ohana* with just enough time to make it inside. But not enough time to lock the door behind me.

I dodged into the den and hid behind the door. I could hear Timo's heavy breathing as he came through the open front door.

"I got no beef wit' you," he said. "Come out. We can talk."

I controlled my breathing as best I could but I knew it wouldn't be long before he'd start searching the house. And the den was the first room on his right. I hadn't had time to notice if he was armed but I knew I should assume he was.

His heavy footfalls echoed on the hardwood floors as he came closer. I thought about my mother's last moments and in a flash of resolve I knew what I had to do.

I waited until his bulky frame threw a shadow in the crack between the door and the frame. Then I pushed the door into his face as hard as I could. Even so, it wasn't enough to knock him down.

"You bitch," he screamed.

Now he knew my position so there was no sense staying trapped behind the door. I jumped out, ready to throw a punch or a kick or whatever I could manage against an opponent twice my size.

His face was smeared in blood. The door must've caught his nose. He looked even more frightening than before but I wouldn't allow myself the luxury of being terrified.

In a display of despicably bad sportsmanship I shifted my weight left, cocked my leg and aimed right for his balls.

Timo went down like a harpooned whale. His howling was so pitiful I felt a flush of guilt but it evaporated when I saw Sunny's Kel-Tec on the floor where he'd dropped it. I grabbed the gun.

"Get up," I said, pointing the gun at him

"I can't."

"Fine. Stay there."

I grabbed my purse off the coffee table and ran to my car. I had no idea where Sunny might be and no clue whether she had just the one gun or an entire arsenal. I stuck the key in the ignition and sent up a little prayer of thanks to the Ford Motor Company when the engine turned over. I bounced down the rutted road and had nearly made it to the gate when I had to slam on the brakes. A police car with lights flashing was blocking my way.

33

Detective Kiki Wong used her onboard bullhorn to tell me to put down the gun and get out of the car with my hands up. I thought the bullhorn was unnecessary, maybe even a little melodramatic, but why have all the bells and whistles if you never get to use them?

I did what she'd ordered.

"You're under arrest," she said as she told me to put my hands behind my back. She clamped on handcuffs. I was surprised at how much it hurt when I tried to wiggle my wrists.

"You have this all wrong," I said.

"Wow, that's a new one," she said. She opened the back door of the cop car and put her hand on my head as I ducked to get inside. She leaned in. "Really. You win the prize for most original comment made during an arrest by a citizen in a starring role."

Once she and her partner had climbed inside, I went on. "No, I'm serious. That wasn't my gun. It was Sunny's. She pulled it on me when I confronted her about the anti-freeze."

At the mention of 'anti-freeze' the two cops glanced at each other. Then Detective Wong's partner, Akuna, turned and looked at me. "Do yourself a favor and save it for the interview, okay?"

We got to the station and Wong and Akuna escorted me to the same room I'd been in the day before. "Don't you guys have more than one interview room?" I said. "Because I've been here four times now and I always get put in this same room."

They chose to read me my rights instead of answer my question.

After a grueling hour of questioning I asked how long I was going to have to wear the handcuffs.

"Oh, my bad," said Akuna. "I forgot." He winked at me as if we were sharing a joke. My wrists were red and starting to swell so the humor was lost on me.

In mid-afternoon they brought me a sandwich and a Diet Pepsi. I hadn't realized how hungry I was until I'd taken a bite. Then I wolfed down the rest of the sandwich in less than a minute.

"You still hungry?" said Wong. "I could get you a candy bar or something."

"How much longer is this going to take?" I'd already told them everything I knew about Phil and Arthur's cover up of the murder of my mom and my uncle Robert. I'd explained about finding anti-freeze under Sunny's kitchen sink and how it pointed to Peggy's unexplained intoxication before her accident and my vomiting that morning. It seemed to me their time could be better served corroborating my allegations than asking me the same questions over and over.

"You're no longer a suspect," said Wong. "We've dropped the arrest and upgraded your status to witness."

I looked around the interview room. "I'm a witness?"

"That's correct."

"I have a degree in criminology, so I know the drill. You can't hold a witness against their will."

"That's also correct."

"Then I guess I will have that candy bar. And I'll buy it on my way out of here."

***

I flew back to Maui without retrieving my overnight bag at Sunny's. I called Steve and he came down and picked me up.

"A lot has happened since you've been gone," he said.

"Yeah?"

"Farrah and Shadow had a falling out. Seems Farrah got in Shadow's face about something to do with Hatch." He looked over at me as if hoping I'd talked to Farrah and could fill in some details.

"What? Don't look at me. I've been on Kaua'i." But I had a hunch I knew what it was about. And bless Farrah. I couldn't wait to see her.

"So anyway, Shadow moved to a women's shelter in Wailuku and she's applied for unemployment benefits."

"Don't you have to have had a job in the first place to get unemployment?" I said.

"Yeah, but she's saying she worked at Farrah's store."

"You're kidding. But Farrah's a sole proprietor. She doesn't have employees."

"Bingo," he said. "So now Shadow's gotten her in big trouble. She told them Farrah made her work off the clock and she paid her under the table. She also claimed Farrah's been doing it for years with Beatrice."

"But Bea just comes in a few hours a week. And Farrah pays her in groceries," I said.

"I know. But the State of Hawaii doesn't see it like that. You're supposed to pay minimum wage, and workman's comp and taxes and stuff."

"Great. So Shadow's gotten her in trouble with the state."

"Unfortunately, that's the least of it," he said.

I looked over and he looked genuinely troubled.

"What else?" I said.

"Shadow's decided she doesn't want Farrah to have Moke after all."

"*What*?"

"Yeah. I guess she called Farrah a bunch of names and said she'd changed her mind."

"But they had a *hanai* agreement," I said. "We had the baptism."

"It's her kid. She can do what she wants."

By then we were approaching Pa'ia. "You want me to drop you at the Gadda?" he said.

"Yes, please."

Farrah looked positively haggard. Luckily, there weren't any customers when I got there. I went behind the counter and gripped her in a tight hug.

"I heard," I said. "I'm so, so sorry."

"I loved him so much," she whispered. "I only had him two weeks but I loved him as if he was my very own."

"I know." Her shoulders shook with her sobbing. I gave her a kiss on the cheek and went over and locked the front door.

Screw the pot-head craving the Snickers bar. This was a family crisis.

***

I called Hatch that night. I wasn't sure how it would go. Could we get through this or had we finally reached the tipping point?

"I'm back," I said.

"Hey, I wanted to call, but… anyhow, did you hear?"

"About Farrah and Moke? Yeah, I heard."

"I feel real bad," he said. "Kind of like it was my fault or something."

"Ya think? She and Shadow were friends, Hatch. You two hooking up was just—"

"What? You think I was doing that? Look, can I see you? I don't want to talk about this on the phone."

"I don't know, Hatch. This is serious. I've just been through hell with this thing with my mother, and now you sneaking around like this. Farrah's my best friend and you've betrayed us both."

"Stop. Let me come up there. I'll only stay five minutes."

"I'm not in the mood for a sales job, Hatch."

"No sales job. Just hear me out. I think I deserve that much."

"How about I come down there? Steve's making dinner for Steven up here tonight and I'd rather talk about this without an audience."

When I got to Hatch's he'd already poured two glasses of wine. "You want some cheese and crackers?" he said. "How about chips? I've got some taro chips around here somewhere."

He looked trashed. Two-day stubble; dark circles under his eyes. His slumped shoulders made him look two inches shorter.

"Okay," he said. "Before you start yelling, let me explain what happened. And then I never want to talk about it again. Deal?"

"Go ahead."

"That girl started coming on to me from day one. When Farrah was here she kept her in line, but after Farrah left, the little bitch put on a full-court press. I told her to cool it and she promised she would."

"I wouldn't call her little lingerie show after the baptism exactly 'cooling it'."

"I know. She was calling my bluff. I'd warned her if she pulled anything in front of my friends I'd kick her to the curb. But she used those kids like hostages."

It added up.

He ran a hand through his hair. "Look, I was stunned when she came parading out like that. You may think I'm just a dumb smoke-eater but I *know* when I'm being played. When you left, I was fighting mad at you."

"Mad at *me*? What'd you have to be mad about?" I said.

"Mad that you had so little faith in me. Mad that you thought I was such a dumb-ass that I'd wreck us for the likes of her."

"I guess I underestimated you."

"Damn straight you did. That girl's bad news, Pali. She may have the right to take that kid away from Farrah, but I've put her name up on emergency services radar. One complaint, one nine-one-one call, one *hang-nail* on any of those kids and I'll have child services on her ass like white on rice."

That was the Hatch I knew and loved.

Making up may be the only upside to a having a fight. But in the right hands, it's the best upside there is.

EPILOGUE

The Kaua'i Police Department got to work unraveling Arthur Chesterton's cover-up of the 1981 murder of Marta Warner Wilkerson and Robert Allen Wilkerson. As it turned out, the mayor got his wish to have his time run out before he could be taken to task. He died of a lung infection before charges were filed and before they could strip him of his pension.

The medical examiner ran a secondary tox screen on samples taken from Peggy Chesterton's body. He determined that although the anti-freeze, or ethylene glycol, markers had vastly deteriorated due to refrigeration, he could reasonably state she most probably had been poisoned prior to her fatal accident.

Sunny Wilkerson was indicted on one count of first-degree murder and a second count of attempted murder. Valentine declined to represent her, citing conflict of interest. If Sunny is found guilty she won't be allowed to collect her share of Phil Wilkerson's inheritance until she's served her time. And even then, probably Peggy's two kids will sue her in civil court for every last dime.

I'm at peace with my decision on what to do with Phil's money. I intend to have a double gravestone made for my mom and Robert and have it placed in the Maui cemetery where Auntie Mana is buried. I'm going to have it engraved, *Beloved Parents of Pali and Jeff.* I figure if I can blow off the stupid name my father gave me, I can also blow off acknowledging our biological relationship.

I'm going to take some of the money and pay off my mortgage and buy myself a new car. Why not? Phil never gave me squat, so the SOB can make up for it now.

I'm going to put the bulk of the money in a trust for Phil's other kids. I've talked with most of them, and, as much as it pains me to admit it, I agree with Phil on one thing: they're spoiled rotten. How does the law describe it? *Fruit of the poison tree?* Yeah, that's them.

Finally, telling my brother Jeff about how our mother died was the hardest conversation I've ever had. I hated telling him on the phone, but I had weddings coming up and I'd blown my airfare budget going back and forth to Kaua'i. His silence made the revelation even harder since I wanted to hug him but twenty-four hundred miles of ocean stood between us.

"I want to come over when you install the gravestone," he said.

"I'd love that."

"And then let's spend a little time together."

"Great. I'll make up the guest room."

"No, I've slept on that nasty sofa-bed of yours," he said. "I think we should get away."

"Get away? To where?"

"I think we should spend a few days in the city."

"San Francisco?"

"No. Who wants to hang out in the fog and rain?" he said. "I'm talking Honolulu."

And so Honolulu it will be.

ACKNOWLEDGEMENTS

Every book begins as a tiny kernel of an idea and grows into a few hundred pages of love, sweat and tears. This book turned out to be a lot of all three, especially sweat, but I thank everyone for hanging in there with me.

My first shout out goes to Roger and Diana Paul. They're big Kaua'i enthusiasts and generous to a fault. Thanks again for everything.

I also want to thank Sam and Ann Densler who trooped along without complaint as I researched every tourist trap and hidey hole on the island. I hope you enjoyed lunch at the Kong Lung Historic Market Center in as much as I did.

Mahalo to Preston Myers of Safari Helicopter on Kaua'i for a never-to-be-forgotten look at the entire island, but especially the bird's eye view of the Pali Coast.

I never tire of thanking my friends, early readers and supporters, including (but thankfully not limited to) Sue Cook, Wendy Lester, Linda Mitchell, KC Spiker, and my dear, long-suffering husband, Tom Haberer.

And finally, a big *mahalo* to my fellow writers at misterio press (no caps, but they're all capital writers) Shannon Esposito, Kassandra Lamb, Kirsten Weiss, Catie Rhodes, Stacy Green, and Kathy Owen.

Please check out our website at
http://www.misteriopress.com
and see the fruits of their labors.

Most of all, a big couldn't-do-it-without-you thank you to YOU, my readers. Please visit my Facebook page "JoAnn Bassett's Author Page" or my website, **http://www.joannbassett.com** and see what's new in the "Islands of Aloha Mystery Series."
Mahalo!

The "Islands of Aloha Mystery Series"
Maui Widow Waltz
Livin' Lahaina Loca
Lana'i of the Tiger
Kaua'i Me a River
O'ahu Lonesome Tonight (coming soon!)

Mai Tai Butterfly
A Maui Makeover Love Story

1

My life ended with a letter bomb. It made for a quick exit, like a magician's trick: now you see her, now you don't. The limb-from-limb pain came later.

At 3:17 on a Thursday afternoon, Mike, our graying hippie mail carrier, plopped a damp rubber-banded stack of mail on my reception desk at All Seattle Realty.

I'm sure of the time because although Mike scoffed at most postal service regulations—picture Ozzy Osbourne doing court-ordered community service—he seemed to pride himself on strict adherence to the mail carrier creed of reliability. He'd clocked his route like a NASA shuttle launch, and the ETA for our office was 3:17p.m., rain or shine.

"Hi, Mike. Got anything good for me in there today?"

"Well, I didn't see anything from the lottery commission, but you never know." He didn't break stride, smiling and clicking me an index-finger salute as he pressed his shoulder against the glass door on his way out. A chill blast of late October wind carried a smattering of soggy alder leaves onto the entry mat.

"See ya mañana, Nola." And he was gone.

The cream-colored number ten envelope hid near the bottom of the stack. It was addressed to my husband, Frank, but as office manager of his real estate company it was my job to open the incoming mail. The letter opener zipped through the back flap with the ease of a scalpel.

I pulled out a single sheet of "Bayside Floral" letterhead. As I unfolded it, a little white card fluttered to the floor. Two handwritten lines in black ink scrawled across the page: *We failed to include the message card with your most recent order. Please accept our apology.*

Pushing back from the desk, I bent over and groped under my chair for the dropped card. As I sat back up, black splotches slid into view, obscuring my eyesight and threatening a fainting spell.

I took a deep breath, squeezed my eyes shut and visualized my carotid arteries expanding to allow blood flow into my brain. I hadn't exercised in months—okay, years—and whenever I felt stressed, or got up too fast, I risked ending up in a heap on the floor.

The dozen or so extra pounds I'd gained since turning forty didn't help either. From the neck up I still looked pretty good—hazel eyes, a straight nose, and a thick mane of curly medium-brown hair. I'd let my stylist talk me into highlights in an attempt to see if blonds had more fun. But the constant pinch at my waistband reminded me I wasn't fooling any salesclerk worth her salt as I flipped through the size sixes on the Nordstrom sale rack.

Opening my eyes, I was relieved to find I could see again. I'd assumed the dropped card was a business card, but it turned out to be a floral enclosure. Printed at the top was a trio of blood-red roses, and below, in my husband's unmistakable spiky left-slanting handwriting, it read: *Thanks for the nooner. You're the best. Love, Frank.*

Nooner? I didn't know normal middle-aged people used that word. Besides, for the past ten years the naughtiest lunch we'd shared involved splitting a slice of banana cream pie. I dropped the card into my purse and zipped it tight. Then I stuffed the high-priced handbag into my bottom drawer and slammed it shut. Didn't help. Even hidden away, that Dooney and Bourke hummed like a high voltage wire.

Frank was sitting in his private office no more than thirty feet from me. The right thing to do was to march in there and demand an explanation. But, on second thought, maybe I should give myself a few minutes to think. I rose from my chair, but the black blotches returned and I plopped back down. Leaning my elbows on the desk, I dropped my face into my open hands. My fingers felt cool against my fevered cheeks. *Deep breath, deep breath,* I silently prayed.

The phone started ringing. The insistent *chirr-chirr-chirr* jangled me into decision mode. Fight or flight? Neither seemed especially appealing.

"Nola? You out there?" Frank yelled. "For God's sake, pick up the phone."

Frank hated answering his own phone. He alleged it made him look small-time if the caller didn't have to wait at least fifteen seconds before he took a call. When I first came to work with him, I didn't believe he'd actually sit there counting, "one-thousand one, two-thousand two" up to fifteen before picking up a waiting call. But that's exactly what he did.

A second line started up, joining the first in a double-time effect. I had to get out of there. Needed some space. I was supposed to ask for phone backup if I left my desk, but I couldn't imagine what I'd say.

It seems Frank's sent flowers to his bimbo and I'm feeling a little woozy. Or maybe, *Frank's been sleeping around during noon hours so I need a minute to go throw up.*

To tell the truth, my brain wasn't as shocked as my heart seemed to be. For months Frank had made long outgoing calls after silently shutting his office door. He'd disappear for hours on end "checking on his listings." For a hotshot real estate broker he certainly didn't seem to care much about being available. He offered all kinds of excuses when I asked why he didn't pick up calls forwarded to his cell phone. Even our son, Frank Jr., a junior at the University of Washington, had commented he'd given up trying to reach his dad by phone.

I made my way to the back door and slipped outside. An invisible vice squeezed my chest as I staggered across the rain-slick parking lot. I approached my beige—or more precisely "desert sand"—Ford Taurus and dropped the keys before I could manage to unlock the door. Bending to retrieve them, I came nose-to-nose with the white magnetic sign on the driver door. It featured a photo of a grinning Frank, alongside his contact numbers and the company tagline: "East-side, West-side, We Do 'Em All!"

I pressed the remote on my car keys. Heard the *peep peep* of the doors unlocking. Fumbling the door handle, I broke a nail but didn't stop to check the damage. I just had to get inside. Shut the door.

In the hush of the snug car I heard my heartbeat drubbing in my neck. I stared through the windshield, reviewing the past few months like a foreign movie I'd been unable to translate.

I'd always figured our marriage to be about average. After twenty-two years it'd taken on a mellow tone—no stunning highs, but no yawning lows either. Frank started the real estate brokerage fifteen years ago, and I'd worked for him for the past ten. I didn't take a salary because what was the point? We shared everything. I figured we made a good team.

Frank wasn't that into sex. Oh, every now and then on a weekend morning we'd sleep in and he'd roll on and off me in about a seven-minute act. Then we'd go out to brunch. I looked forward to the brunch part.

But last month while looking up a market analysis for Frank I'd clicked on his Internet "history" section. In the drop-down list, it showed URL's like "hotlove.com" and "sockittome.com." We had a bunch of practical jokers in our office so I'd figured someone had sent them to him as a gag. I'd even chided him about it.

"Yeah," he'd said. "Brad—you know, the new guy from California—attached a couple of porn sites to an email he sent me. I clicked on them without thinking. Wow, there's some pretty graphic stuff floating around cyberspace."

His face had darkened. "You know me, Nola. I'm a solid family man and I expect the same of my agents. I probably should have a chat with him about office protocol. No more goofy stuff on the company computers. Besides, those sites carry viruses." He'd scowled as he gravely thanked me for bringing it to his attention.

The cell phone in my purse began chiming. I fished it out and stuffed it in the center console to smother the sound. Then I turned the key in the ignition, backed out of the parking stall and aimed the car for home. Good thing the car knew the way. I had no idea how to get there.

I pulled into the driveway and pressed the opener button on the visor. The garage door lurched up in a creaky 'welcome home.' Once safely parked inside, I hit the button again and the door slid back down. I turned the key to off and listened to the *tick, tick, tick* of the cooling engine. It was spooky in the dusky gloom of the three-car garage, but I felt cozy inside the warm car. Like being the smallest in a set of *matryoshka*—those Russian nested dolls that get smaller and smaller one inside the next—I had layers and layers of protection buffering me from what lurked outside. My breathing slowed, warmth returned to my fingers, and I tilted my seat back to rest my eyes for a moment before going inside.

After a minute or so, I felt ashamed. I'd leapt to a pretty damning conclusion based on rather flimsy evidence. Besides, I wasn't some ingénue catching her boyfriend out behind the bleachers with the school skank. Middle-aged men stray. It doesn't mean they don't love their wives. I wanted the facts, but first I needed to calm down so I wouldn't come off sounding like a shrew.

I rehearsed the call I'd make as soon as I'd gotten a grip. First, the office phone would ring about twelve times before someone finally picked up.

"Is Frank there?" I'd say.

"Sure, Nola. He's been really worried about you." Whoever answered would want to chat, but would realize Frank was anxious to know I was all right.

I'd wait on the line the required fifteen seconds.

"Darling, where are you?" he'd say. *"I've been going nuts here. Are you okay?"*

"Yeah, I'm fine. But I need to ask you about something."

"What's wrong, honey?"

I'd tell him about the flower card. He'd launch into a perfectly plausible explanation about Brad being up to his tricks again. He'd be furious about the forgery, and would want to fire him for unprofessional behavior—not to mention causing me major mental distress.

I'd admit that at first I'd been upset, but after thinking it over I realized it was just a bad joke. Then I'd say I didn't think he should let Brad go over a juvenile stunt, but he should be put on notice because he'd seriously breached the rules of acceptable office conduct.

Frank would commend me for my sensible attitude and offer to take me out to dinner—anywhere I'd like to go.

Feeling much better after coming up with a credible scenario to explain the smarmy little card in my purse, I took a deep cleansing breath, hunched my shoulders into the back of the car seat, and drifted off.

***

When I awoke, I panicked for a couple of seconds before remembering why I was dozing in my car in the shadowy garage. Sitting up, I opened the car door. The overhead light came on and the alarm dinged to remind me my keys were still in the ignition. I turned the key. The lights on the dash sparked to life.

The digital clock glowed 5:32. Anxiety shot through me as I did the math. I'd been gone for two hours and hadn't called in. Frank would be worried sick.

I dug out my cell phone and dialed the main office number. Sunny, a mortgage broker Frank had brought in to do in-house loans, picked up after two rings.

"Hey, Nola," she said. "What happened? You didn't tell anyone you were leaving."

"I know. I felt really sick all of a sudden. Sorry."

"Well, Frank said to put you right through if you called. Hold on. I'll see if he's still here."

I started counting. Frank came on the line after only four seconds.

"Where the hell are you? We had clients out front and no one to greet them. You know you're not supposed to leave without getting someone to cover for you."

Not exactly the greeting I'd imagined. Probably best to hold off mentioning the florist card until he got home.

"I didn't feel well so I came back to the house."

"That's no excuse. What's the problem?"

"Uh. I'm not sure. I just felt sick and needed to come home."

"Since when do you just waltz off the job and leave me in the lurch? Maybe you haven't noticed, but I'm trying to make a living here."

"Make a living? So, tell me, does that 'living' include buying flowers for your nooner girlfriend?" I honestly have no idea why that popped out of my mouth. I felt my cheeks heating as I waited for his reply.

"What the hell are you talking about?"

"In today's mail you got a note from Bayside Floral. They were returning a message card that said, 'Thanks for the nooner.' It was signed 'Love, Frank,' and it sure looked like your handwriting." I prayed he'd launch into an outburst of indignant fury.

Instead, he granted me the decency of a long pause before saying, "We need to talk."

That remark ranks right up there with *There's been an accident* or, *We've found a lump.* Just four little words and yet when I heard them, I knew my life—as I'd known it—was over.

Made in the USA
Las Vegas, NV
12 September 2021